Byker Grove
Turning on, Tuning in

BYKER GROVE
TURNING ON, TUNING IN
Don Webb

BBC BOOKS

BYKER GROVE is a
Zenith North Production

Published by BBC Books,
a division of BBC Enterprises Limited,
Woodlands, 80 Wood Lane, London W12 0TT

First published 1990
© D Webb 1990
ISBN 0 563 36067 4

Set in Baskerville by
Goodfellow & Egan Ltd, Cambridge
Printed and bound in England by
Richard Clay Ltd, St Ives Plc
Cover printed by Richard Clay Ltd, St Ives Plc

CONTENTS

CHAPTER ONE

Marilyn Charlton was her real name. But it wasn't the name she would have chosen and it certainly wasn't the name she used. Except for Miss Hagger, most people knew her as Charlie and that was good enough for everyday use even if Uncle Steve persisted in calling her his beautiful blonde Marilyn. Uncle Steve was definitely creepy though, and not even a proper uncle. He lived with Aunt Sophie and she was Charlie's mum's sister but they weren't married and people lowered their voices when Charlie was in the room and his name came up. But his creepiness to Charlie was more due to the fact that he flicked her skirt up when nobody was looking. Most other males stopped doing that after senior infants and the fact that he laughed every time he did it didn't make it any more of a joke. So she wore shorts when she could and kept out of his way when she was dressed for school. And she never took a lift off him to go anywhere.

Looking out of the window at the rain which was battering the flowers in the back garden, she hummed a little tune. This was the day, right enough, and it hadn't come any too soon. Denton Burn had had it and so had Greg. Charlie was fifteen and on top of the world. She didn't care who knew it and if Greg didn't want to know it, Greg could blow off on the breeze. She turned away from the window and looked at herself in the mirror. One spot was all that was left of a mammoth chocolate binge a fortnight ago and she poked it gently before brushing her hair.

The Byker Grove kids had looked interesting at the football match. And the leader, Geoff, had been jolly even though they had been snotted by Denton Burn. The Denton Burners had behaved like football hooligans, jumping up and down and directing sneers in all directions. She hummed the tune again and sang a few bars to herself thoughtfully. She kept on humming as she dressed especially carefully in her new silky baseball jacket and got her trainers out of their box. Then she twirled in front of the mirror until her mother shouted from downstairs.

'Marilyn! Bring your sheets and your duvet cover down!'

Charlie grunted to herself and gathered up the bedding. When she went into the kitchen, her mother looked at her critically.

'Why do you have to dress yourself like something off a cornflake packet?' said Mrs Charlton. 'What's wrong with a dress once in a while? You've got nice legs. It's not as if you had to hide them, is it?'

Charlie groaned audibly. Her mother continued. 'And never mind the big groans. You're not too old to have to stay in.'

'Mum!'

But the telephone rang and the argument didn't get a chance to form into a full-scale thunderstorm. Although it could have, Charlie admitted to herself later, as she shot down the path and away to freedom of a kind even if she did have to keep her head down against the rain. But by the time she had bounced to the end of the road the rain had stopped and a watery sun had started to struggle through the clouds and make the roofs shine. And Charlie's spirits, which never stayed low for long, began to rise in time with the dance step she practised as she rounded the corner on her way to the bus stop.

It was still raining, though, further over in town. In New-castle itself, the rain was having a good time rattling the windows of a train which had stopped on the high-level railway bridge just before completing its journey from London. Beckett rubbed his hand against the window and looked out. The place was deserted, not like it had been all those years ago when he had first seen it. No boats in the docks, only a restaurant-type floating disco thing. No smoke either, and no noise, except for the wind and the banging rain. He stood up and picked up his briefcase. The only other man in the first-class carriage looked up and tried a tentative grin. Beckett looked back at him till he stopped smiling. Then he went out into the little anteroom between the coaches, went into the lavatory and looked at himself in the mirror. He looked like what he was, a businessman. He looked confident, reliable and trustworthy. Which just goes to show that you can never tell by looking at someone what they are. Because Beckett was a criminal and it was crime which had brought him to Newcastle. Not crime as in hitting people on the head and taking things away from them but crime as in moving large amounts of money around very quickly, and when the music stops there's not as much money left as there was in the beginning.

And that was exactly the problem that Geoff was facing at Byker Grove. As always, the petty cash box had been locked in his desk, which had itself been locked with a key which he never let out of his sight. None of which stopped him being ten pounds short in the box and, as this was the fourth time something similar had happened, Geoff was not best pleased. In fact, Geoff was raving, jumping, seething mad.

Mary O'Malley came in and looked at him. She nodded to herself without saying anything, put down the cup of tea she was carrying and went out again. Geoff shook his head and put the cash box back in the desk drawer. The door opened again and Dexter stuck his head in. Geoff was not at all sure about Dexter. Dexter was the temporary replacement for Gwen who had been sent on a course to make her better at dealing with people and Dexter had been sent down by the Recreation Department. As far as Geoff was concerned, Dexter was all mouth and trousers.

'Haway, Geoff, man!' said Dexter chummily.

Geoff looked at him coldly but the look rolled straight over Dexter's back. He gave Geoff a matey grin. 'So. What's the big word?'

'What big word?'

'What do you want us to do?'

Geoff thought about this and managed to dismiss the faintly off-colour thought which sprang to mind. He jerked his head and led the way out, Dexter hopping along beside him.

'What do you do all day when there's no kids here? Bit cushy, isn't it? More like a bobby's job, this is.'

The more Dexter talked, the less Geoff liked him. But then he remembered why Gwen had been sent on the course and he kept his mouth shut. There was plenty of time to sort Dexter out. Plenty of time.

'Come on over round the back and you can meet Brad, give him a hand,' grunted Geoff. 'He'll keep you out of trouble, I shouldn't wonder.'

'Who's Brad? I thought there was just the two of you here.' Dexter grinned. 'This really is a bobby's job, this is, no danger. Three people, your own kitchen and I haven't seen one kid yet.'

Geoff turned and looked at Dexter, who held up his hands in apology. 'Just joking, Geoff man, just joking!'

But Geoff's gaze didn't relent. Eventually he nodded and led the way to where Brad was unpacking his van, taking out some rolls of black material. Brad turned and looked at the newcomer. 'Who's this?'

'Dexter Dutton. He's come down to lend a hand while Gwen's away on the course,' said Geoff, with a remembering frown.

Brad clearly knew all about it. 'Aye. Right. She made a right pig's ear of that vet business with Spuggie, that's for sure.'

Dexter looked from one to the other and waited for somebody to explain what had happened with Gwen and Spuggie, whoever she was. Geoff looked at him. 'What?' he demanded.

Dexter shrugged. It wasn't his business and he already

10

had the uneasy feeling that Geoff didn't like him. Lots of people had difficulty with Dexter's manner although there wasn't really any malice in him. He was young and brash and shot his mouth off all the time. None of them hanging offences, true, but none of them designed to make him popular with older people, either. He looked at Geoff again and made the wisest decision he'd made that day. He said nothing.

'Right,' said Geoff. 'Come down the office and let's square the paperwork off. Get you started properly. See you later, Brad.'

And he led the way, Dexter trudging behind, thinking that maybe it hadn't been so bad at the Town Hall after all. Still, he brightened a little as he thought of the afternoon. There'd be bound to be some lasses about, somebody to try his chat-up lines on. And, although Geoff obviously didn't care for him, Geoff didn't have eyes in the back of his head. But maybe he didn't need them.

Geoff turned and looked at Dexter suspiciously. The next question was unexpected. 'How old are you, anyway, Dexter?' Geoff said, looking at him. Dexter was mystified. Geoff repeated the question. 'How old?' 'Me? I'm twenty-one, me. Twenty-one and fancy-free. Well . . .' He grinned a little sheepishly. 'I'm not exactly free. But I'm very reasonable.' He looked hard at Geoff, trying to guess why the question had been asked but Geoff had turned away and was stalking off down the corridor. Dexter hurried to catch up.

'Is it important how old I am?' he asked.

'Only I need to know how much you're going to cost my budget, that's all,' replied Geoff. 'I still have to pay for Gwen, even though she's on a course.' He looked at Dexter. 'Maybe I'll see if I can manage without you.' Dexter nodded briefly. It was what he was used to. His longest time in any one section so far had been eight days. Geoff was already regretting his decision to ask for cover for Gwen. In fact, he wasn't entirely sure he should have sent her on the course either. Even though what she'd done had caused so much trouble and heartache all round.

Fraser was still pondering the same question. He looked at Spuggie as she sat at the breakfast table, her head down and her face still showing the signs of the tears that had nearly broken his own heart as he had lain awake in the middle of the night. He walked across and touched her hair but she jerked her head away angrily. He tried his best to make her see that the vet's job wouldn't have been possible anyway.

'You've no jeans, you've no wellingtons, even your T-shirts are in rags. How could you work in a vet's place?'

Her face worked and she almost spat back at him. 'They were going to pay us, Fraser! You know nothing, you don't. You think you do but you're all talk. You just don't want me to do anything with me life.' She rested her head on her hands and looked down at the table. He tried to touch her hair again but she jerked her head away once more.

'You'll be late for school if we don't go now,' he said.

'I'm bunking school,' was her sullen reply, her face set in that stubborn way he hated. He breathed out slowly, trying to be as patient as he could, but his heart started to pound at the thought of what might happen.

He fought against the sick feeling. 'You can't bunk school. We can't have the truant copper round here with me mam sick.'

Spuggie blazed back at him. 'I don't care. I don't care about school or the copper or me mam or him or you or anybody. Leave us alone!'

He breathed out, trying to stay calm.

'Just get your name on the register, then.' She looked at him and then nodded once with her head down. 'Then you can clear out, no bother,' he said, putting his arm round her as they left the room. She flinched angrily away from him at first but he felt her relax a bit as they went across the landing to the top of the stairs. She even waved cheekily at the beady

12

eye behind the spyhole in Mrs Next-Door's door. As usual, their nosey neighbour was watching to make sure that those Campbell children were still living up to her worst fears, being young and noisy and alive.

By the time they got to school, Spuggie was already working out how she was going to get her name in the register to say that she'd been there all day, so her mother wouldn't have to open the door to the truant policeman. And then she started to think about how she was going to spend the day.

Charlie's day was already set in concrete. She could see Greg waiting with his hangdog face, every line of his body telling her that he knew what she was going to say and that it just wasn't fair. Charlie was his girl and she had no right telling him it was all over. She wondered grimly what little goodbye present he would have brought her to make sure she knew exactly how lousy she was being.

She didn't have long to wait. He took her arm as she walked past and held on tight enough to stop her pulling it away. 'It's over, Greg,' she hissed at him, knowing that Anna Dixon was watching it all, eagle eyes flashing, waiting to pass the news round at break.

'I know it's over.' He stopped and looked at her. 'I just thought I'd give you these. You were keen enough a week ago.'

He searched her face for a reaction as she looked at the two tickets and the leaflet. Then he smiled. The effect was just right. Dismay and pleasure were chasing each other across Charlie's face. The tickets were for the karaoke competition at a local club and she'd been bending Greg's ear for a fortnight about having a go, even though privately she'd thought she'd have been about as likely to do a karaoke turn as take her shorts off on the Metro in the rush hour. She looked at Greg and he nodded at the tickets. 'Seeing as you were so keen, I got you these tickets. You might just as well have them even so.' And the sneer she hated so much came back into his voice. 'Maybe you can find a boyfriend at Byker Grove to take you,' he finished.

Charlie looked at his stupid one-up-on-you face and remembered how he had put her down the first time she'd told him her secret ambition. He'd laughed and spat chips all over the top deck of the bus.

'You?' he'd spluttered. 'A pop singer, you? Give us a break, will you?' And he'd told Anna Dixon, who'd told the rest of the North-East. She looked at the tickets again. Then she smiled.

'Oh, Greg! Thank you!'

She stretched up on tiptoe and kissed him on the cheek. Anna Dixon's eyes went round like pinwheels. Greg looked sick. And Charlie carried on. It's very nice you're not jealous. Because there *is* a boy at the Grove and he has asked me out but we didn't know where to go.' She waved the tickets and the leaflets. 'But you've solved everything. It's really nice that you've been so big about it even though we have finished.'

And she skated into the yard, followed by Anna 'Big Ears' Dixon, whose tongue was tripping her up as she tried to find out what was going on. She snatched the leaflet off Charlie. 'What's this?' Anna demanded. 'Karaoke? What's karaoke?'

Charlie smiled sweetly at her. 'It's singing to backing tracks. It's how a lot of singers get started, as a matter of fact.' And she carried on into the reception area with its smell of disinfectant and ancient cabbage. But today the smell didn't matter. Today was the first day of the rest of Charlie's life and it was looking better by the minute.

Not that you could say the same for Robert, who was being hoisted into the Ironside wagon on the other side of town to be taken to school. Life looked exactly the same to Robert – dreary. And Speedy didn't make it any better, hopping from foot to foot as if he wanted to go to the toilet. Robert looked down at him.

'What's up with you, Speedy?' he asked. 'Have you got two legs in one knicker or what?'

Speedy grimaced at the ambulance guy, who was fussing around with the chair, preparing to swing it into the ambulance.

'It's all right, Speedy, man, you can talk in front of Igor,' Robert reassured his friend. Speedy grimaced again but the ambulance man took the tension right out of everything by pretending to be a hunchback. Crouching down with his knees bent and holding his knuckle to his forehead, he lurched close to Speedy, who lurched back quickly.

'Ah, the bells, the bells, master!' said the ambulanceman. Speedy backed away nervously.

'Get off!' said Speedy. 'Get off!'

The ambulanceman turned away as he fixed the last bits of the wheelchair. 'Aha, Jim lad!' he grunted, twisting his face up into a very weird expression indeed. Speedy looked at Robert.

'You might as well tell us,' said Robert. Speedy nodded.

'I just don't want you to forget, that's all,' said Speedy. 'Don't forget, you won't need this lot this afternoon. I'm coming to get you from school.'

Robert looked a bit puzzled. 'Speedy, I know you're coming to get us. You've told us three times this morning already. I'm crippled, you know, not stupid. And don't forget about Radio Rocket, will you, either? We've only got half an hour to do the whole transmission, the whole test and that's if Winston remembers to brings his tranny.'

'I know, I know. I'm going to remind him,' Speedy said crossly.

The ambulanceman came back from the front of the truck in slightly more normal public servant mode. 'Finished, girls? Got your date fixed up, have you?'

He nodded reprovingly at Speedy. 'And I don't want you bringing a yellow orchid this time neither. It'll clash some- thing terrible with his complexion.'

Then he got into the ambulance and went off to pick up the next customer. This was Old Mr Bennion who would keep Robert amused all the way to school talking about the state of his joints. Amused is actually too strong a word to use here. But when Mr Bennion is in full flow the word Robert uses to himself is distinctly unprintable. These are the times when Robert really wishes he hadn't hit his head on the goalpost. And if he really had to hit his head on the goalpost, when Old Mr Bennion is on fine form and in full flow, Robert occasionally thinks it might have been a good thing if his skull had shattered like a ripe melon. This kind of feeling doesn't last all that long though, unless Old Mr Bennion is smoking roll-ups.

Speedy pedalled his way to school, pretending to be Tommy Simpson, the greatest Englishman ever to ride in the Tour de France, who actually died in the saddle. But the weather wasn't wet enough to feel suitably miserable so Tommy Simpson didn't last all that long. After one or two changes, Speedy burst into the schoolyard as Joey McLoughlin winning the Milk Race, and nearly mowed Winston down in the process. Having been almost minced, Winston didn't much feel like talking about his transistor radio. But Speedy soon persuaded him, first by being very persuasive and, when that didn't work, by being bigger.

This was nearly always the argument that got to Winston when he was on his own and he finally agreed to bring his radio to the Grove. They needed Winston's tranny because that very afternoon they were going to get their pirate radio station, Radio Rocket, off the ground in more ways than one. They were going to broadcast a test transmission and they were going to do it from the roof of Byker Grove.

All this was faintly illegal but, as P.J. had pointed out, so is robbing banks and that happens all the time. The argument stood up only bcause they wanted to run a pirate radio. It would not have stood up against a really reasoned examination. And, apart from anything else, they couldn't pass the

16

time playing table tennis because the table tennis table was out of action, which was almost an entire reason on its own. If Winston brought his tranny they could listen to their test transmission because none of them fancied asking Geoff to listen out on the set in his office.

What Beckett did, as previously mentioned, was emphatically criminal and far more criminal than running a pirate radio station even though 'steady citizen Beckett' was often heard to make rude remarks about the youth of today. If they did as he had done in his youth, he was fond of saying, and if they had gone to school with a positive attitude and had gone to night school with the same sort of dedication, there would be fewer single-parent families and there would be less sponging off the state. He was never actually heard to say that there would be less crime. He was lots of things, was Beckett, but, to be fair, he wasn't a hypocrite.

He'd come up to Newcastle upon Tyne (and he'd smiled to himself every time he'd heard a local emphasise the 'upon') to make a lot of money for himself and his friends and then he was going to go away again and nobody was going to see Beckett in this particular place again.

The job itself was simple. He was to go into a local businessman's office and give them all the papers he was carrying in his briefcase. The businessman was going to give him, in return, a lot of money and Beckett was going to get back on the train and go away and pretend to be an honest accountant for the rest of the year. In fact, to be fair to Beckett again, for the rest of the year he *would* be an honest accountant. In fact, if you wanted to split hairs, the only really dishonest period of Beckett's year would be the ten minutes or so he was going to be in the office. Ten minutes out of a year isn't bad. Or wouldn't have been.

Beckett whistled his way into the ground floor reception area of the building which had a lot of floors and was very modern and was in the town centre which, Beckett was surprised to see, was pretty well set out and pleasant, considering all the horror stories he'd heard about this so-called deprived area. He looked around and the girl at the reception desk smiled at him sweetly.

'Can I help you, sir?' she said, also sweetly.

He nodded and showed her his letter of appointment. This meant that he didn't have to say anything. Little pitchers have big ears and there was one little pitcher by the window, reading his newspaper and looking out of the window. He was obviously not interested in Beckett at all. In Beckett's experience, that kind of little pitcher had the biggest ears of all. The girl at the desk told him which floor to go to and kindly pointed out the lift.

'Thank you,' said Beckett and made for the lift. At the last minute, though, he didn't get in the lift which was standing obligingly at the ground floor with its mouth open. He walked round the corner instead and stopped for a moment. And he found out just how big the little pitcher's ears were.

Out of sight, round the corner, looking out of the window, the little pitcher said, quite quietly, into his little radio. 'He's going up the stairs!'

But Beckett wasn't. Beckett was going out of the window and jumping down to the ground and running like hell. There wasn't going to be any dishonest ten minutes this year for our Mr Beckett. This looked like being one of the most honest years he'd had for some time. His heart was beating very fast and the sweat was coming through his clothes, even though he wasn't running. He looked at his watch like a man late for an appointment, and concentrated on walking through the surprisingly well-laid-out streets of Newcastle, past the well-favoured and smiling people, and made for the railway station.

When he got to the station, he stopped. Newcastle is an open station. This means that you don't have to have a ticket to get on to it. This also means that if there are policemen talking to all the people going on to the station then something is not quite right. Beckett turned and walked away. He walked fairly slowly for two reasons. He needed time to think, that was the first reason. And the second reason took him back to his days at school and his brother, who he hadn't thought of in a good long time. If you've done something wrong, his brother used to say, walk, don't run. And Beckett thought of this advice and thought of his brother as he walked the streets of this northern town which was beginning to feel like a prison. And his brain began to go round in circles and his feet itched to do what they mustn't. His feet itched to run.

In Spuggie's case it was different. If she didn't run, she might not get away with it. It was bad enough sitting at the back of Four Eyes Finnerty's class waiting for your name to be called out and then make a break for the outside. It was even worse when you knew your interfering best friend had already got wind of the fact that something was up and there was no way that dear little Bridie would keep her great gate shut if she thought she could make trouble for —

'Kirstie Campbell!'

The sound of her name made Spuggie shoot upright and she forgot to say 'Miss' and old Four Eyes peered out at the class. 'Does anybody know where Kirstie is today?' she asked and there was a muffled snigger. Not all that muffled, really, and Spuggie knew she'd gone bright red, the kind of bright red that only goes with red hair. She held her hand up.

'Here, Miss,' she said and shot a fierce look at Bridie. 'Shut up, you,' she told her.

'I wish you'd pay attention, Kirstie,' wittered Miss Finnerty and then turned her attention to the rest of the class. Bridie tugged the back of Spuggie's blouse and Spuggie wrenched it away bad-temperedly.

'You bunking off, Campbell?' Bridie hissed.

'No! I am not,' said Spuggie in a fierce whisper.

'Wait for us,' said Bridie 'and I'll go with you.'

Spuggie gritted her teeth at this and kept her head low, cursing Bridie with unladylike thoughts.

But it all worked out in the end. Bridie was sent for. Nobody knew why but the general opinion favoured Nitty Norah, the nit nurse, whose car had been seen in the car park. They had to ask your mum and dad before they could go scritting through your hair, though, which was why you were discreetly nicked out of class so that anyone'd know why.

Spuggie waited a few moments and then took off while Miss Finnerty was peering in her desk. She was out of the gates like a little whirlwind and off down the street. The day was hers, even if she still hadn't actually decided what to do with it. The sun came out and little white clouds came over against the blue sky. Spuggie could feel her spirits rising by the minute and she had to really fix her mind on feeling miserable, otherwise the whole bunk-off would go to waste. Not much use disappearing to show everybody how lousy she felt if she got in a good mood by accident and spent the whole day laughing. It didn't take long to get her misery back, though.

Without thinking about it, she found herself going towards the Grove. As she walked along Platt Street she saw a flock of dirty, fleabitten pigeons nodding and pecking as they looked for their dinner outside a chip shop. She felt in her pocket and counted the few bits of change she had. There wasn't even enough for a bag of chips and she charged into the pigeons as if it was their fault. They beat up into the air until she went past and she wasn't more than a few yards past them before they were down and pecking again.

Stopping outside a petshop, she looked at the puppies tumbling about in the window, four of them in a huge cuddle with floppy ears, trying to bite and wrestle at the same time. She kneeled down and pressed her forehead against the cold glass to watch them. Suddenly her eyes filled with warm, wet tears and she gulped hard to keep the lump down in her throat. She stood up quickly and wiped her eyes with the hem of her jumper. Then she saw the reflection of a policeman in the window. He was looking at her and started to cross the road. But a car went past and stopped him and she was round the corner and gone, tiptoe down the alley and away.

Then she was near Byker Grove. A couple of big, heavy spots of rain fell and a curl of thunder made her wince. She didn't like thunder. She didn't like lightning either, and a fork suddenly shot down the sky in front of her. She counted three and the thunderclap came hard, nearly overhead. She ran like mad into the Grove grounds. Then she stopped, seeing Brad and Geoff unloading black stuff out of a van. She crouched down by a bush so that she could hear what they were saying. Now she was Spuggie the girl spy and secrets were what she was after.

'What do you reckon?' Geoff asked Brad. 'D'you think you'll have enough or what?'

Brad shrugged. 'Can't tell,' he said. 'No idea. Knowing these kids, I'll need to black in the little vestibule as well.'

Spuggie waited till they were looking the other way, then edged round the corner of the grey stone wall, and out of danger. As she leaned back against the wall a cat came up, its tail high in the air. Spuggie grinned and bent down towards it. But it skipped out of her reach, teasingly, and gave a high, cross miaow. She followed it round the far corner, fingers pressed to her lips. Girl spies needed to be quiet.

'Puss, puss, puss,' she said, as quietly as she could. The cat looked at her, flirted its tail and disappeared. It looked as if it had gone right through the wall. She couldn't believe it.

'Puss, puss, puss.' She went quiet again. Then, as she crept forward, Geoff's voice right behind the wall threw her into a panic. Geoff was very hot on people not bunking off and he was even hotter when people bunked off and went down the Grove in school hours.

21

'There's somebody round the back,' said Geoff and she could hear him walking towards the corner. Panic-stricken, she suddenly saw where the cat had gone. She followed, quick as a flash, sliding through a window half above and half below the ground, tugging her skirt down behind her as she went.

Brad and Geoff came round the corner and Geoff scratched his head, puzzled. 'Probably someone in one of the gardens,' said Brad. 'Aye,' said Geoff. 'Funny, though, it sounded nearer.' And they went back round the corner, leaving Spuggie to catch her breath and see where she was.

She was in the cellars of the Grove by the look of things and a right creepy place it was too. She looked at the window, ready to climb right out, but the thunder clapped again and the cat talked some more so she turned round to make the best of things. The cat weaving to and fro behind her, brushing against her legs, made her feel a bit better and she became the girl spy again, hiding in the cellars of the enemy headquarters, ready to rescue whatever needed rescuing. After a minute or two, she decided that they could all rescue themselves. Because the cellars stank. She wasn't sure what it was they stank of exactly, but she wasn't going to hang around and find out. She went back to the window and, wouldn't you know it, Geoff was stuck right outside, talking to Brad about the World Cup. He looked round as the cat jumped out of the window and made him jump too.

'Close that window, will you, Brad?' she heard him say. 'That's all we need, a cat bog in the basement.' Brad closed the window. The girl spy quietly said a very rude word. And hoped there was another way out of the cellar.

Which, after some blundering about in the dark, she found, by way of some very uneven stone steps which led to a long, thin door. She bent down down and listened. Not being able to hear anything, she pushed the door open slowly. She peeped out and found she was in a corridor. Then she aimed for the stairs and made it just as Mary

O'Malley and Alison came into the room below the landing. Lying on the floor, her face grew hot and cold in turns as she heard them talking about her. They were being kind but it was none of their business and she wanted to stand up and shout at them to tell them so. Which would have done no good at all, so she just had to lie there and listen to her own sad story.

Mary started. 'That poor little mite. Nicola told us what happened.' Alison was a bit puzzled, by the sound of her voice. 'What *did* happen?' she said. 'The last time I saw Gwen, there were no problems.' 'Well,' said Mary and paused. She was revelling in it, of course, being Mary O'Malley. 'You know it was all fixed up for Spuggie to go and work at Gwen's brother's the vet's?' She paused and Alison nodded. 'Well, when it came time for her to go and do it, they'd got somebody else.' Alison was shocked and the disbelief was there in her voice. 'No!'

Mary nodded importantly. 'Oh, aye. They said she was too young.'

Alison said, 'I don't believe it. Has anyone said anything to Geoff?'

Mary's reply was grim and to the point. 'Oh, yes. Where do you think Gwen is now?' And without waiting for a reply, she went on. 'Geoff's sent her on a course to learn how to deal with people and to learn how not to upset young kids.' They went out through the door and Spuggie crept along the top landing to where she could hear Geoff and Brad coming in. Somebody else was with them. Spuggie craned her neck as far as she could. It wasn't anyone she knew.

It was Dexter Dutton, as a matter of fact, master of putting his big flat foot in it and just about to do so again. Brad and Geoff were talking about the darkroom arrangements and Geoff paused to introduce Brad and Dexter. They nodded at each other, neither one liking what he saw. Brad saw Dexter as a mouthy punk, Dexter saw Brad as a long string of nothing much at all. And he'd seen him

23

skateboarding down the path. Skateboarding came a bad second to a Bros concert as far as Dexter was concerned. And a Bros concert was just a bit better than having both legs taken off without being put to sleep first.

'Brad's building us a darkroom,' said Geoff.

Dexter brightened. 'Oh, aye,' he said. 'I'm all for that, man. The body beautiful. Suits me!'

Brad scowled at him. 'We're doing landscapes at the moment,' he said.

It rolled off Dexter like water off a duck's back. And he grinned cheerfully at Brad. 'No offence, man, like,' he said. 'Whatever turns you on, I always say.' He grinned again.

There was a little silence.

'What does Dexter do?' said Brad, after a bit. 'Whatever I tell him,' replied Geoff, 'I hope.' This broke the mood which had been getting grim, and they laughed. Geoff went on. 'He's here till Gwen gets back off the course.'

Brad nodded. 'Be some human relations in this course, will there? How not not to crush kids' hopes and feelings possibly?'

Geoff grunted and nodded. 'I shouldn't wonder,' he said. Then he clapped Dexter on the shoulder. 'Haway, Dexter, show us what you're made of, man. I need a window putting in.'

Dexter grinned again as Geoff led him off. 'I'm good at that, me,' he said. 'I've been putting windows in since I was about six.'

Geoff looked at him. 'Aye, right. But in this case, I mean replacing them, not smashing them to smithereens.'

Dexter nodded. 'Whatever turns you on, Geoff, man.'

They went out. And Spuggie went on and up to the very top of the Grove, finally walking along a corridor with a step up at the end and a rickety wooden door. She tugged and tugged on it only to be terrified almost witless as the door opened and a flurry of pigeons flew up right in front of her. She slammed the door shut, annoyed with herself for being such a wimp. 'Only birds,' she muttered under her breath. Damn birds, she thought to herself. And, then, down below, there were voices and footsteps. She plunged into the nearest room in a panic and slammed the door as Geoff and Dexter appeared in the corridor. Peeping out through a crack, she saw them walk along to the roof door. Geoff slammed it shut.

'Damn thing,' he said. 'Wind's always blowing these damn doors.'

And they ambled back down the corridor. Spuggie peeped out till they were out of sight, then opened the door very cautiously. Just as she did, Dexter peered quickly round the corner. She froze as their eyes met. Dexter looked at her, then grinned and winked.

He grinned to himself again as he walked down the corridor. Kids, he thought, you couldn't tell kids what to do. That was the art of being a kid, not doing what you were told. Time enough for doing what you were told when you'd left school and gone to work. He pulled a face and Geoff caught him at it.

'What's up with you,?' said Geoff. 'My old war wound,' said Dexter, starting to limp. Geoff shook his head as he finished explaining the Byker Grove rules. In particular, kids weren't allowed on the premises until four o'clock and that was it. Dexter grinned to himself and thought of the little red-haired kid. If there were any more like her at the Grove it might not be a bad place to spend a few days, after all. And that mood stayed with him all day, even when he broke the window he was putting in and Geoff told him his fortune, which didn't have a lot of good stuff in it.

The good stuff came in a bit later on though, and it was called Alison and it had legs that went on forever till her waist stopped them. She looked in to offer them both a cup of tea, asked for Brad, smiled and went out. Dexter looked at Geoff and whistled but Geoff looked sour.

'Your mouth's leaking,' said Geoff. But Dexter didn't mind. Geoff was too old for that lovely lady.

'I wouldn't mind going in a darkroom with her and seeing what developed,' Dexter quipped.

Geoff nodded and looked at him sourly again. 'She's spoken for.'

'Pity,' said Dexter, but his grin didn't go away.

'Come on down the kitchen,' Geoff answered. 'If Mary O'Malley's tea can't take your mind off sex, nothing can.'

And off they went and the tea wasn't nearly as bad as Geoff had said although the constant chatter that went with it was a bit wearing. But Dexter just shut his ears to that and thought of the lovely Alison, who was apparently spoken for by Brad. But nobody falls for someone who rides on a skateboard for pleasure.

And while they sat drinking their tea, Spuggie slipped out like a will-o'-the-wisp. And the cat sat on the wall and washed its whiskers and watched her go.

Beckett, in the meantime, had been very lucky all the way round town. He wasn't dressed for catching buses. People of his age and general appearance didn't often get on a bus. And he remembered his dad's old saying, if you're over thirty and you're on a bus, you're a failure. It hadn't come home to him till now. He'd as soon have been sitting on a bus as walking. He thought about getting a taxi out to the airport but if the police were as smart as they had been so far, the airport would be covered with people looking for him and taxi drivers have radios and they can talk to central control and they might have been warned to look out for a well-dressed man in his forties, looking worried and carrying a briefcase full of forged mortgage papers.

He had a cup of coffee in a busy cafe but had to leave that when it got less busy and the woman who wiped all the tables was beginning to look at him as if he shouldn't be there. So he got up and left no tip to teach them all a lesson and started to walk the streets. But then the thunder and rain started and he was up against it. Two of the three telephone boxes he went past were smashed, and the third needed a phonecard which he didn't have and he really had to ring Sammy because what he needed was a car to take him out of this benighted northern town which was beginning to feel more like a dungeon by the minute. And then the rain, which had been toying with him up till then, decided to get serious and started coming down like stair rods.

He was near a deserted allotment and he went to the far side, broke the lock on a shed, got inside and sat on a box in amongst the cobwebs and the smell of old vegetables. How about if you were over forty and in a dirty shed full of sacks? How much of a failure were you then? The rain stopped drumming on the roof of the shed. He looked out. If he couldn't make the telephone call himself, maybe there was a friendly native who could help out.

And then he saw a scruffy little red-haired kid poking a frog with a piece of straw. The frog jumped and the kid giggled. Beckett smiled in spite of himself. It was that sort of giggle. Looking around, he could see there was nobody about. He walked across the allotment until his shadow fell across the frog and the little girl looked up.

Spuggie had a weakness for frogs. It wasn't a serious weakness, they just made her laugh. It was something in the way they crouched, as if they were expecting a clip round the ear then they jumped with a great burst. But they didn't go far. She wasn't tormenting the frog, just teasing it along a bit. But when the shadow first fell across the frog and then across her, she thought it might be the RSPCA. And she put the straw down quickly. She stood up.

'I was only tickling it,' she said, a bit guilty. The man looked at her. 'I can see that,' he said. 'I can see that. Hard to resist, aren't they, frogs?'

She nodded. Then she took a more careful look at him, at the way he was dressed and the briefcase he was carrying, and a sudden thought made her stomach sink. He looked just like somebody official. Just her luck, she thought. First day she'd bunked off for months and straight into a truant officer from the council.

'I'm off sick from school today,' she offered. 'I've – er I've had a toothache.'

She showed him the tooth she had been saving for this kind of situation. It had a little bit knocked off it when she fell off the skateboard. He looked at it with interest. She held her mouth open.

'Mm,' he said, this truant officer with a bit of a twinkle in his eye. 'Does it hurt much?'

She shook her head. 'Not much, not now,' she told him. She looked at him hopefully to see if he had fallen for it. He nodded slowly as if he was thinking what to do next.

'What's he going to do about it?' he asked. She was startled.

'Who?' she said. He looked at her again and this time she could see the twinkle in his eye and she thought, oh dear, he's not falling for it.

'Well, the dentist, that's who,' he said. 'That's where you've been, I expect. Considering you've had a day off school, that's bound to be where you've been, I should think.' She nodded.

'So, what's he going to do with it?'

She thought rapidly. It was a long time since she'd been to the dentist and she improvised as much as she could. 'He's put a dressing on it,' she said, confidently. 'And I've got to go back tomorrow to get it finally fixed up. Yes, that's it,' she said.

'And you're on your way back to school now, aren't you?'

She nodded again.

'Do you know what I think?' the stranger said.

Spuggie shook her head but she did know what he was thinking and she was right. 'I think you're playing truant, that's what I think,' said the tall man with the smart suit and the briefcase and Spuggie's heart sank into her boots. This was what Fraser had warned her about and this was what she had hoped and hoped wouldn't happen. She shouldn't have bunked off. And now she was caught. It wouldn't have been much of a problem normally. She went to school pretty regular and so did Fraser, who was keen not to end up like his dad. But Spuggie's mam hadn't been too good lately and she was drinking too much of that stuff she called tonic wine but which Fraser and Spuggie both knew wasn't tonic wine. It just made her sick and gave her a headache. And Spuggie's dad had gone out a couple of months ago and just hadn't come back. And if this rotten truant officer went round to the house, he'd see that their mother wasn't well and he'd see that there was no father and hadn't been for some time, and if he couldn't see it nosey Mrs Next Door'd soon put him right. And the flat wasn't too clean, neither.

Spuggie looked at the truant officer and her stupid eyes started to fill up again with tears. The man's face changed and he knelt down beside her.

'Hey,' said the truant officer. 'Hey! Don't cry. I'm not a truant officer, you know. I'm not a truant officer.' And he gave her the biggest handkerchief she'd ever seen to wipe her eyes on. And he told her to blow her nose on it. She looked at it doubtfully.

'I can't blow me nose on this,' she said. 'It must have cost about two pounds, this. Haven't you got a tissue?'

He shook his head and laughed and the twinkle became very merry. 'Use it,' he said. 'It was a birthday present. I didn't have to pay for it.'

Then another thought came to Spuggie. If he wasn't a truant officer, what was he? And what was he doing talking to little girls in the middle of an allotment?

'Don't worry,' he said quickly. 'Here!' And he showed her some cards and another thing with his name on. 'I'm harmless. But I do need a favour.'

She looked at him very doubtfully. 'What?' she said.

He took her hand and looked around. 'Come over here a minute. I just want you to run a message for me.'

She let him tug her along a little. He was looking over his shoulder. Before she knew where she was, she was inside the shed and looking at him fearfully. But he just sat down and looked at her.

Spuggie looked at the door and then again at the man. He shook his head and smiled. 'Don't worry,' he said. 'Don't worry. Nothing bad is going to happen.' And she suddenly knew she could trust him.

'Are you all right? What's up?' said Spuggie. Because the man looked old and tired and, underneath the twinkle, Spuggie saw something in his eyes that she hadn't seen in a grown-up's eyes before. He was frightened. He looked at her and nodded again.

'All I want you to do is go and get me something to eat. And then I want you to make a telephone call for me. Do you know how to make a telephone call?'

She looked at him scornfully. 'Course I do. What do you think I am, a cripple?' she said.

He shook his head. 'No. No, I don't think you're a cripple. I think you're a truant but I don't think you're a cripple.'

She thought about what he had said and an idea suddenly struck her.

'Are you a spy?' she said. 'Because if you are, I'm not helping you.'

He laughed and his face cleared. 'No. No, I'm not a spy. Now, if I give you some money, can you go and get me something to eat?'

She nodded and held her hand out. He gave her a banknote. When she looked at it, she saw it was a twenty-pound note.

'Haven't you got nothing smaller than this?' she said. 'It's going to cause a right stir, me going into a shop with a twenty-pound note.' He looked in his pockets again and came up with a fistful of change and a five-pound note. All together, it added up to about eleven pounds. She stood up importantly.

'Right,' she said. 'What do you want? And who do you want us to phone?'

Taking some paper out of his pocket, he gestured at the box for her to sit down. 'I'll have to write it down,' he said. 'It's quite a complicated message.'

She sat down, feeling very excited. Whatever it was that was going to happen it had to be better than Four Eyes Finnerty and geography.

At the Grove, things were hotting up. Alison was trying to avoid Brad. And P.J., Speedy and Robert were roasting Winston, who had forgotten to bring his radio yet again. The arrangements for the trial broadcast of Radio Rocket were almost ready but they couldn't test it without a radio of their own.

Winston blustered and argued and promised but they just ignored him and concentrated on the next problem which was how to get Robert and his wheelchair up on the roof. Eventually they did it, with a lot of cursing and puffing.

'What if it rains?' said Speedy, looking around. 'What if it doesn't?' said P.J. and they left the matter there.

Winston wandered off and found Kelly and Mary O'Malley discussing times past. Kelly rolled her eyes at him and he found himself asking her to go bowling. This was a shock to Kelly but she said yes. It was an even bigger shock to Winston who'd never asked a girl out in his life before. But he looked at Kelly's smiling face and felt good about it.

Downstairs, Brad made his usual pass at Alison, who lifted her head, looked at him coolly and invited him to go bowling too, leaving him reeling from the shock.

And Marilyn Charlton, Charlie as now was, walked up the path to the Grove, feeling excited and terrified at the same time. She jumped about a foot as a car swept past, aerial flickering and horn sounding a rude tune. Then she stopped and watched, fascinated, as a *very* young girl got

31

out of it and, giggling, held her skirt down against the wind before waving the car goodbye and shooting off up the path.

'Wicked!'

A voice behind spun Charlie round and she saw a friendly black girl with big, happy eyes, 'Hello,' said Charlie and cursed herself for sounding feeble.

'Love the jacket, honey,' said Hayley.

And they made friends and went inside and Charlie felt a good deal better.

Not so Alison, who'd watched thirteen-year-old Debbie Dobson getting out of the flashy car. She caught Debbie giggling about it with Kelly.

'But who was it?' said Kelly, eyes flashing with curiosity behind the glasses. Debbie tossed her head and flicked her a sideways glance. 'Come on Debbie! Who?'

Debbie giggled again. 'Michael. Or Wayne. I'm not sure. They all work at the supermarket. They fancy our Nicola something rotten.'

Alison didn't really hear any of this but she had a pretty good idea of what they were talking about. She took Debbie away with her for a little chat. Debbie's bottom lip came out but Alison was determined to have her say.

'I'm not stupid, you know,' protested Debbie. 'I'm not a child. I can spot a dirty old man a mile away.'

Alison shook her head. 'They're not always old and they're not always dirty,' she said.

'But I know them,' Debbie insisted. 'I know them. They're friends of our Nicola's.'

Alison shook her head again. 'It doesn't matter if you know them. You can't tell who is likely to harm you. I don't want to get heavy but you must never put yourself in a position where your choices are taken away from you.'

Debbie's eyes grew round and solemn as she took the message in.

Then Fraser came into the room and looked around. 'Anyone seen Spuggie?' he asked.

They all shook their heads. And there was a burst of laughter from outside where Dexter was talking to Hayley and Charlie. Fraser's head turned. 'Who's that?' he demanded. His manner was spiky.

'It's Dexter,' said Alison. 'He's here in place of Gwen.'

Fraser nodded and his face grew stern. 'Got rid of her, have they? Good riddance to bad rubbish!'

Alison stood up crossly. 'That's not a very nice thing to say, Fraser,' she began. But Fraser rounded on her and his voice made the room go very quiet.

'Gwen promised Spuggie that job, Alison,' he said bitterly. 'Then she whipped it away.'

'You're taking this all the wrong way,' said Alison, her face flushing. 'It's no reflection on Spuggie.'

Fraser looked at her, weighing his words before speaking. 'Alison,' he said. 'Have you ever had something taken away from you when all you have to look forward to is nothing?' He paused. 'Have you?'

Alison's head went down.

'I didn't think so,' finished Fraser.

And he went out.

But, as far as Spuggie was concerned, the vet's job could go hang. She was having a great time. Beckett had given her a lot of money and she'd gone to the little shop on the corner and bought all sorts of things. Then she'd dragged the bag back to the allotment, crouching from bush to bush, and back to the shed.

Beckett had been convinced she was never coming back. Anyone watching as he dragged her inside would have rung the police on the spot, but nobody was and nobody did.

And so she sat on a box and ate three packets of crisps, a bar of chocolate and two potfuls of strawberry yoghurt with her finger because she had no spoon and she listened to Beckett talk while he ate. He drank from a can of fizzy orange.

'I couldn't get any beer,' she told him. 'I'm too little to be eighteen.'

He nodded and smiled and talked away. His voice fascinated her, going up and down in strange places, and she told him so. He wasn't cross and ruffled her hair. She snatched her head away but, secretly, she was pleased. And then he looked at his watch and told her to go home because it was late and people would be looking for her.

Spuggie looked at him scornfully. 'Me?' she said. 'Looking for me? Nobody looks for me. Nobody cares where I am.'

Then she went, and later on, lying in the old hut on some sacks, Beckett thought about what she'd said and hoped it wasn't true.

When she got home, Fraser was waiting for her and he was cross. She had a bag of chips for him and one for herself and a big bag of stuff from the supermarket where she had spent the rest of the money Beckett had given her.

'Where did you get the money to buy all this?' he demanded, opening the bag.

'I can't tell you,' she said, going on the defensive. 'I thought you'd be pleased instead of moaning and shouting.'

He looked at her long and hard. 'If you've robbed if off someone, Spuggie,' he said slowly and carefully, 'we'll have to go in care. And *I* don't want that, even if you do.'

But Spuggie was saved from having to answer. Just then her mam came unsteadily out of the bedroom where she had been lying with a headache. She looked puzzled when she saw the groceries but her face soon cleared.

'Ah, pet, thanks for going down the shops,' she said. 'See?' she added, looking at Fraser. 'I said your dad wouldn't leave us with no money.'

And she took some eggs and started to make something for tea.

Spuggie looked at Fraser and went into her room. Fraser switched on the television.

The Metro Centre was a good place to go in the evening, full of light and colour and things to do. If you had some money, that was. Winston had conned enough off his dad to take Kelly bowling. And Duncan had pinched enough out of Geoff's cash box to last an hour or so and when that went he could borrow off Carl.

As for Brad, well, he met Alison and they went bowling as she had promised.

He also met Mike. And that was a bit of a surprise. Because Mike was the man that Alison lived with. And that wasn't at all what Brad had had in mind.

Over in the allotment, Beckett slept fitfully on his sacks. Spuggie dreamed of Beckett and the stories he had told her. Charlie sang herself to sleep. Robert went to sleep slowly and then sat up quickly in the middle of the night, convinced his accident had been a dream. Until he saw the wheelchair like a steel spider in the middle of the room.

Debbie Dobson, on the other hand, was trying not to go to sleep. Because she was afraid of the man she'd seen on the video, with knives where his fingers should be. And the house creaked around her.

CHAPTER TWO

The next day the sun shone down hard enough to crack the flags, as Mary O'Malley would have put it. Mary was Debbie's and Nicola's and Jemma Dobson's granny and she had been feeling very much like a spare part until she had started lending a hand with the kitchen and the teas down at the Grove. It had taken years off her, she was keen to explain to everybody she met. This didn't make up for the fact that it had changed the Dobson girls' lives too. Their special hideaway, where they'd once been able to get away with all sorts of things, wasn't quite the same with Gran around. But, to do her justice, Mary would no more have split on anything the girls did at the Grove than she would have thrown bricks at the Pope.

When Debbie had gone to sleep the night before, it had been in spite of herself. And it was a relief, when she woke up, to find that she hadn't been cut to little pieces in the night. After a night like that, going to school was a bit of a relief.

For Charlie, school was a necessary evil, until she could get on with the real business of her life which was singing. Taking the tickets for the karaoke competition out of her desk, she looked at them once again just to make sure that they were still real. She only just got them out of sight before the teacher looked up with bright, suspicious, teacher's eyes to catch her out.

Spuggie didn't like school. But she went. She'd go along with anything that meant she could carry on helping Beckett. And that meant staying out of trouble until four o'clock.

The rest of them coped with their day as well as they could. Beckett probably had the worst of it, sweltering in the hot shed as the sun beat down. He also found that fizzy orange wasn't all that good at quenching thirst. His little friend had had no luck with the telephone call. He just had to hope that she'd come back. As he waited, he played a game of chess against himself, using the folding set and board in his briefcase. Chess was Beckett's passion. He'd always wished that people could move with such precise and particular beauty. It was his search for this precision and beauty which made him take risks such as the one which now had him stuck in an allotment shed in Newcastle, waiting for a spirited red-haired urchin with a happy grin and sad eyes.

Meanwhile, at the Grove, Geoff was almost literally hopping mad. He had just unlocked the cash box which had lost yet more of its contents. He was also having to listen to Mary O'Malley's cross-making brand of advice. He wasn't sure which was worse.

'You should lock it up,' she said.

'I do lock it up,' he replied through gritted teeth.

'If you locked it up,' she carried on remorselessly, 'there would be no chance of money going missing, would there?' And she nodded wisely to make sure that he took her point. He stopped and looked at her. 'What?' she said. Geoff controlled himself as best he could.

'If,' he said, speaking calmly and reasonably, 'I lock my box every day, if I lock it up and turn the key and put it in the desk and lock that and shut the office door and lock that too, how can thirty-seven pounds go missing?'

Mary O'Malley nodded wisely again. 'You can't have locked it up safe,' she said. 'Otherwise it wouldn't have gone missing. Maybe,' she said, warming to her theme, 'maybe there's another way into your office and the desk and the box and you just haven't spotted it.'

He grinned at her. 'You've been watching Miss Marple again.'

'Better than watching Newcastle get beat,' was the quick and accurate reply. Anything was better than watching Newcastle get beat. But before he could answer, the door burst open and in walked the new kid with the fair hair and the eyes that seemed to go twice round her head, they were so bright. Geoff couldn't help grinning at her.

'Geoff,' she said and then stopped.

'Right so far,' Geoff replied. 'Why stop when you're winning?'

Behind Charlie appeared Hayley's smiling face.

'Geoff,' said Hayley and stopped. Geoff waited as the two girls looked at each other and giggled.

'Karaoke,' they both said together.

'Granted,' said Geoff and they both pulled faces and rolled their eyes and started talking at the same time. By the time Geoff had calmed them down, he was nearly as excited as they were, even if he didn't know what they were talking about and certainly didn't know where to get what they wanted. Which was a backing track to sing against at a competition and which they would use to promote the name of Byker Grove. If he would get it.

'Geoff! Please!' said the two of them and Geoff was lost.

He stepped into the corridor to see Debbie walking down the end of the Grove with Kelly's arm round her shoulders. Seeing Mary on her way to the kitchen, he nodded at the two figures. 'What's up with your Debbie?' he said. Mary shrugged.

'See if you can find out, will you?' And Mary went off on her mission, while Geoff took Hayley and Charlie off to see if he could make any sense of karaoke.

Being wise in the ways of little girls, Mary knew there was no point asking straight out what was wrong with Debbie. She listened outside the door and heard enough to make her hair stand on end. Kelly was telling Debbie not to worry, it was only a picture. But Debbie's forlorn little voice replied, 'It's all right sitting here now in the light talking about it. But it's different when the light's out and the heating goes off and the house starts making noises.'

There was a little pause and Kelly said, 'What film was it, this?'

Debbie spoke hesitantly and it was clear that the film was real to her. 'It was the idea of it,' she said. 'There was this man and his fingers were like knives. And he can get in your dreams. And while he's in your dreams, he can cut you to pieces with his finger knives. So all the lads and lasses have to stay awake.'

There was a little pause, then she finished in desperation, 'But they can't!'

Mary stepped swiftly into the deep silence to see Debbie and Kelly staring at each other with big, round eyes. 'Right,' she said. 'Where have you seen a picture like that?'

Debbie was quick off the mark. 'It wasn't me, Gran. I haven't seen it. There's this girl at school and her brother got it out the video shop and made her watch it.'

Mary looked at her, knowing that this was a load of rubbish but not knowing how to get the truth out of her. Dexter Dutton broke the spell by coming in through the door, large as life and twice as ugly.

'Never fear, Dexter's here.'

Mary O'Malley looked up and the girls made their escape. Mary eyed Dexter and checked her watch.

'You're a bit late, aren't you?' she commented, as the door shut behind the two girls. Then 'ever had the feeling you weren't wanted?' she said. Dexter's reply startled her a little.

'I was born with it, Missus,' he said bitterly. Then he grinned at Mary and took the sting out of it. 'Take no notice,' he went on. 'It's been a bad day. Started badly and got worse.' She wasn't fooled and made him a cup of tea.

Geoff had been having a good time with Hayley and Charlie. He smiled as they chattered away, finally discovering what they really wanted and having to scratch his head all over again. Dexter came in on the end of the conversation with a cup of tea for Geoff. He also had the name of a little record company run by a mate of his who might be able to get a backing track for the girls, provided it wasn't Pavarotti.

Hayley and Charlie were suitably impressed. So was Geoff, until he caught Dexter gazing at Charlie's retreating figure. When he heard Dexter muttering under his breath, 'For you, Charlie, anything!' Geoff wagged a finger at him, 'That child, Dexter, is fifteen years old. And don't you forget it.'

Dexter said that he wouldn't and went off. Luckily for him, Geoff couldn't see his crossed fingers.

Spuggie arrived home in a tearing hurry, ready to rush off out again but Fraser was home before her. Their mother was lying down with a headache in the bedroom – she said she was cold. While Spuggie was filling the hot water bottle, Fraser said he thought they should get the doctor but Spuggie reminded him that the doctor hadn't come the last time because it wasn't an emergency.

'How does she look?' Fraser asked, sounding worried.

Spuggie rolled her eyes. 'She looks like she always looks when she's been doing this, Fraser. She looks sad and she looks sick. You'll have to look after her. I'm going out.'

'She'll be all right,' Fraser said. 'I'm going down the Grove now. Why don't you come with us?'

Spuggie gave him a scornful look, then went back into the bedroom with the hot water bottle. When she came out she was holding an empty bottle of wine. Fraser took it.

'I don't go down the Grove now,' she said. 'I've better things to do.'

Fraser nodded. He knew why Spuggie didn't want to go to the Grove. 'Gwen's not there,' he said. 'She's gone on a course.'

Spuggie looked at him pityingly. 'What makes you think I care about Gwen? What makes you think I care about any of them?' And she carried on getting ready to go out.

Fraser picked up the wine bottle, carried it to the balcony and let it drop. He watched it smash on the ground below. A dog prowling around in the rubbish sniffed the pieces of broken bottle. And a woman pushing a pram looked up and then walked on. Fraser went back inside. Spuggie was horrified.

'That could have killed someone!'

'It's killing me mam,' he said coldly. 'Why shouldn't it kill someone else?'

There was nothing left for Spuggie to say. She hurried out.

At the Grove, there was a great air of secrecy. To everybody's surprise, Winston had finally remembered his radio and was standing holding it in the radio room. But, being Winston, he was still arguing. His mother was sometimes heard to say that Winston would argue with himself to keep in practice. He stood and argued with P.J., Robert and Speedy.

'I don't see why it's got to be me,' he objected.

P.J. accused him of being chicken. Speedy wagged his arms and squawked like a pregnant hen. Robert spun idly in his wheelchair, scoring imaginary goals. Radio rooms were not Robert's scene but they'd do till he could walk again. Till he could run again and he flashed down the right wing on to Gazza's through ball and whipped it across to where Lineker . . .

They were all looking at him. P.J. spoke first. 'Are you in this, Robert, or what?'

Robert nodded.

'So you've got to be in the corridor, blocking the way with the —' Speedy stopped lamely.

'With the cripple wagon. Right?' said Robert, making them all feel bad. He started wheeling himself to the door. Speedy followed.

'There's no need to be like that,' said Speedy. He hated Robert being in the wheelchair — he still remembered the way Robert could play football. Robert flickered a grin at him.

41

'Yes, there is,' said Robert. 'I'm a poor weak cripple, remember. I've still got to get down the Metro with me mouth organ and tin cup to get a few pennies together.'

Speedy smiled with relief. His friend was having him on, not for the first time. Robert stationed the chair in the corridor and Speedy went back to where the argument between P.J. and Winston had reached a peak. P.J. was almost hopping up and down by now.

'It's got to be you, Winston,' Speedy interrupted firmly.

'Why?' said Winston, his bottom lip jutting out.

'Because you won't lend anyone else your radio, dummy!'

Winston considered this and eventually had to agree. 'All right,' he said. 'What do you want us to do?'

The idea was that Winston should take his bike and his radio and spin round various locations so that P.J. could broadcast a Radio Rocket test transmission and they could find out what the reception was like and how far they could reach.

P.J. explained this slowly to Winston.

'I might get caught,' objected Winston.

'We'll come and visit you in Kirklevington,' said Speedy.

Kirklevington was a youth custody centre just outside Darlington, which they all treated with a healthy respect. Speedy knew a lad who'd come out of there with a tattoo. Winston thought about the possibility of ending up in Kirklevington, until P.J. pointed out that you couldn't get in trouble listening to a pirate radio, only running one.

'But I *am* running it,' said Winston. 'I'm running it with you lot.'

'Well, Winston, m'man,' said P.J., dropping back into Eddie Murphy land which was a good sign. P.J. only used jive talk when things were going well. 'If you don't tell anyone, sweet thing, we won't!'

'Aye, right,' said Winston. 'Mind you don't.' And he was off on his bike, radio tuned to the right frequency and held firmly to his ear.

P.J. sat at the console and switched everything on. His eyes gleamed as he looked at Speedy.

'Let the good times roll, Speed, m'man,' said P.J. And he slotted the jingle cassette in and held a thumb up. Speedy grinned back. He was strangely excited, like in the first few feet of a hairy fun fair ride, when it felt as if he'd left his stomach behind.

Winston swept out of the car park and nearly killed Geoff, who was talking to Dexter. He screeched to a halt, skidding on the gravel.

'Hey up,' said Geoff. 'Watch where you're going.'

Winston nodded, said he was sorry and shot off again to the sound of loud crackling on the tranny.

'Where are you going?' Geoff shouted after him. 'And get that damn radio tuned properly!'

But Winston was beyond normal thought. Swooping down the path with the wind in his hair, he was nearly as excited as Speedy. But he still couldn't hear anything. He rounded the corner and cycled along behind the Grove wall.

Back in the radio room, Robert stuck his head through the door, wanting to be part of it too. He looked at his watch and so did the others. The same thought had occurred to them. Winston must be in position by now.

'Give him a couple more minutes,' suggested Robert. Speedy rushed to the lookout window. 'I'll see if I can spot him,' he said.

But Geoff had already spotted him. He had walked down to the wall and looked over it to see Winston off his bike and with his radio pressed to his ear. When he spoke to him the effect was unusual, to say the least. Winston jumped about three feet in the air, spinning round at the same time.

'Winston, man, what are you up to?' said Geoff, puzzled. He wasn't sure he wanted to know but he had to ask. Winston looked all round for inspiration. The radio went on crackling. 'I'm playing hide and seek,' he said eventually.

Geoff nodded at the radio. 'I should turn that off if I was you, then. You'll get found in minutes.'

Winston nodded, switched it off and shot away, counting in fives. Geoff watched him go and wondered, not for the first time, if he wouldn't have been better off down a pit. At least he would have had some redundancy money by now.

Winston cycled on, looking for somewhere a bit more private.

Speedy couldn't see him at first from the lookout window. Then he spotted Winston's spiky head sticking up above the wall. He shot back to the radio room where P.J. was spinning and jiving and ready to go. He stuck his head round the door and his thumb in the air.

'He's there,' said Speedy and P.J. went on the air. The jingle rang out, followed by the patter.

'This is Radio Rocket, your friendly station, the first with the news, the first with the hot platters and the cool rap, tune now to Radio Rocket and points west.'

Winston was knocked to pieces, hearing the words through his radio. He stood up, his face a picture of delight, and aimed thumbs up at Speedy who was hanging out of the window. Speedy thumbed back and disappeared to tell P.J. and Robert the good news.

'Can he hear us?' demanded P.J.

When Speedy nodded yes, they all shook hands, P.J. giving the high five and leaping in the air.

'Tell him,' said P.J., 'to get on his bike and see how far away he can pick us up.'

Speedy was just about to rush out of the room when he realised there was a better way. 'You've got the mike,' he said. 'You tell him.'

'Right on,' agreed P.J. and leaned into the mike.

Winston got the message and made like the Flying Dutchman. He was soon right on the edge of a council estate and Newcastle was laid out in front of him under the afternoon sun. Newcastle could have been under attack by Godzilla for all Winston knew or cared. He leapt off his bike and squatted in the gutter, all his attention on the radio and the sounds pouring out of it.

'Once again,' came P.J.'s voice. 'For those of you who didn't hear it the first time, here's our jingle.' He played it and Winston listened, his face a picture of delight. It was then that he got a nasty shock. It came from behind and it put the fear of God in him.

'Hello, young man,' said PC Grant. PC Grant was the local beat copper. Winston stood up and looked at him. P.J. played the jingle and PC Grant reached out a hand and took the radio from Winston's nerveless fingers. He looked at it and smiled.

'They're good, these, aren't they?' he said. Winston couldn't get enough spit in his mouth to actually say anything but just smiled hopefully and nodded. PC Grant looked at him.

'Are they expensive?' he asked. Before Winston could try for some spit, the jingle stopped and P.J. started again. This time, to Winston's horror, his words were a bit more direct.

'Enough of that rubbish, anyway,' the radio said. 'Are you receiving me, Winston? Are you receiving me loud and clear?'

PC Grant looked at the radio and then at Winston, with a puzzled expression. Then his face cleared. 'Ah!' he said. 'Right. I've just realised what's going on.'

The silence stretched and Winston waited. He couldn't decide whether to burst into tears or force himself down the nearest manhole.

'Have you?' he squeaked. 'Aye,' said PC Grant. 'It's that Steve Wright in the afternoon, isn't it? Mr Spoo-oo-oo-ns! He makes me laugh, he does.' And to prove it, he laughed. Then he gave Winston his radio back and went away. Winston switched the radio off and sat down in the gutter until his knees stopped wobbling.

*

45

Some time before this, Spuggie had reached the allotment. Beckett was still there and she told him about the phone call and how the man hadn't been there. But the woman had said she should ring again later. Beckett nodded and there was a long silence. Spuggie thought about the question she had decided to ask him but she couldn't be sure whether or not to ask it. She looked at him and he caught the thought behind her eyes.

'What?' he said, smiling. He looked like a wolf, Spuggie thought, and she shook her head. But suddenly, before she knew it, her mouth asked the question anyway.

'What did you do?' she said and immediately wished she could take the words back. But he just smiled again.

'What did I do? What did I do that makes me cower in a hut in an allotment and depend on the kindness of strangers? One little stranger, as a matter of fact. One strange little Spuggie.'

'You must have done something. Why won't you tell us what you did?' she said. He grinned at her. He did look like a wolf, she thought, but a very kind wolf.

Beckett said, 'Maybe it's a crime so revolting that you won't help me any more. Maybe if I tell you why the police are looking for me, you will turn white and rigid and disappear shrieking through the door to summon the forces of law and order and they will apprehend me.'

Spuggie looked at him solemnly. 'If you're not going to tell us,' she said, 'all you've got to do is say so. I'm not bothered.'

He nodded. 'I'll tell you one day. I'll write to you from South America and tell you what terrible crime I committed.'

Spuggie thought about this and she had a better idea. If he was going to South America, he could take her with him and she could learn to do the lambada. She told him and he laughed a lot before falling silent. Spuggie knew what this meant. He wasn't taking her anywhere and he didn't know

46

how to tell her. She didn't care. She was having an adventure. She could worry about it being over when it was over. Up till then she was having a good time. It was a lot better than drinking Mary O'Malley's tea at the Grove and listening to P.J. pretending to be Eddie Murphy. She looked at Beckett's folding chessboard.

'What's that?' she asked. He looked at it in surprise, having forgotten all about it.

'This?' he said. 'This is a chessboard. Why? Do you play chess?'

'I've never tried. Is it hard?'

He showed her the pieces and she picked up the king.

'What does this one do?' she wondered aloud. He took it from her and held it lovingly.

'This is the king,' he explained. 'Male, restricted, nervous. He can only move one square at a time. In any direction, mind, but hesitant, not sure of himself.'

One by one, he picked up the rest of the pieces and told her about them, all through the long afternoon in the allotment hut that smelled of vegetables. He told her about the pawns, the poor infantry, always ready to lay down their lives for the more important pieces. He told her about the queen and the bishops and the rooks which could sweep like broadswords through the ranks of the other side. But the pieces that caught Spuggie's eye were the knights, like little horses with arched necks and flashing eyes. And when he said what they could do, how they were used, she really fell in love with them.

'These are the ones that make sense of a crowded arena,' said Beckett, watching her rapt face. 'They can hop, skip and glide to make room for the heavy artillery.' And he told her about the queen, the very opposite of the timid king. He told her that the queen can go where she likes. 'If I'm the king, Spuggie,' he said. 'You are my queen.'

Spuggie smiled a clear and brilliant smile, and tugged at

47

her grubby T-shirt and jeans. 'Why, aye, man,' she laughed 'I'm the queen all right. In all me robes. Some queen.'

She touched the chessboard lightly. Then 'Will you teach us to play?' she asked longingly and he nodded.

Through the long afternoon, he taught her how to play and, to his amazement and delight, she absorbed the very feel of the game, her little shining head bent close over the board and her eyes turning to him with delight every time another point became clear, every time she scored a little success.

While Spuggie was finding out what a lot of fun it is to learn something new, Charlie and Hayley were discovering what a real pain in the bum a bunch of bored lads can be. They'd found a disco record of 'Jimmy Mac', stuck it on the player and were practising for the karaoke competition. But P.J., Speedy and Winston had decided that the act needed a little something extra and were doing a Bananarama-type male disco turn behind them. Debbie and Kelly were almost helpless with muffled laugher when Charlie turned the record off and stood with her hands on her hips.

'What's the matter, sweet thing?' P.J. said. 'What's going down? You want to take a walk on the wild side with little old P.J. here? Take it and shake it, you foxy chicks.'

Charlie and Hayley gave them a withering look.

'Don't hold your breath, P.J.,' said Hayley and they both went out.

P.J. shrugged at the others. 'Listen,' he said. 'It's not my fault if they're not ready to be cool.'

'All you're doing, P.J.,' said Winston, hitting the nail on the head, 'is waiting till you're ready to shave.'

Hayley and Charlie were having a conference of war in the passage when Robert appeared. 'Make way for Robocop,' he said as he tried to squeeze past. But then he got wedged against a chair and Charlie went to help. His face was cross as he struggled but when he looked up and saw

Charlie he smiled and it was a nice smile. Charlie grinned back and suddenly felt a little light-headed. She'd gone across to help a poor cripple, doing her Florence Nightingale bit, only now it was turning into something different. She stood and looked at Robert and he sat and smiled at her. Hayley got the hint.

'I'll be in the kitchen,' said Hayley and disappeared. They didn't even see her go.

'Can I give you a hand?' said Charlie.

'How about the use of your legs?' said Robert.

Charlie couldn't believe what she found herself saying next. 'It all depends what you want to do with them,' she said, going pink.

Robert smiled again as she manoeuvred his wheelchair free. 'I'm a bit limited, like, with the wheels.'

But her answer was quick and to the point. 'You'll not be in there forever, though, will you?' she said.

He shook his head and grinned again. 'No,' he said, 'I will not.'

She gave him her very best smile. 'That'll be something for both of us to look forward to, then,' she said and shot off to find Hayley before she did something really stupid. Like throwing herself on top of him. She grinned at the thought and felt herself going redder and redder as she raced down the passage.

Robert couldn't quite believe what he'd heard either, and rolled after her as quick as his arms could move the chair.

Meanwhile, in the office, Geoff was looking grim. Cash box in hand, he said to Alison, 'I'm going to have to get the police in, damn it!'

'Are you quite sure?' Alison replied.

'Positive,' said Geoff. Then Brad stuck his head in through the door, Alison looked a little flushed, and Geoff decided to make himself scarce. 'Fill Brad in, will you, Ali?' he said, and went.

There was a brief silence.

49

'Do you suppose that was tact?' said Brad. Alison smiled. 'I think it might have been,' she replied.

'I enjoyed myself at the bowling last night,' Brad began. 'Mike's a nice lad.' There was another little pause before Alison spoke. She was not quite sure where all this was leading. But Brad didn't leave her in doubt for long. 'It's just a pity,' he said.

'What is?' asked Alison and Brad smiled a wicked smile. Moving round in front of her, he rested his hands on her hips. She made a slight movement to get away but his grip was just firm enough to stop her.

'He's going to be very lonely when you leave him and marry me.'

The silence between them stretched and Brad lowered his head to Alison's. Her lips parted. Then the door opened and in rattled P.J., Speedy and Winston, jostling and pushing each other. P.J. was the first to speak. 'Can we borrow Geoff's ordnance survey map?' he said. Alison slid out of the circle of Brad's arms, took the map out of the desk and gave it to P.J. There was an embarrassed moment and Brad raised his eyebrows. 'Is there anything else we can help you with?' he said. They all shook their heads and started to leave. Just as they went through the door, P.J. fired his parting shot. 'Sorry we interrupted you!' The door closed behind them and Alison and Brad heard the explosion of giggles from outside. He went towards her again but she shook her head.

'No what?' said Brad. 'No anything,' said Alison but there was a certain speculative gleam in her eye and just the trace of a smile at the corners of her mouth. Brad settled for that for the time being.

Outside the office, Geoff found the raucous bunch whispering amongst themselves. They immediately arranged their faces into blanks. As he reached for the door knob, Speedy said, 'Just cough before you go in, Geoff, I should.' And this set them off again. Geoff looked at them and shook his head, then lifted his hand to knock at the door. But before he could, out came Alison. 'It's all right,' she said with a twinkle. 'We managed to get our clothes on when we heard you coming.' And she swished off down the passage. Brad came out and Geoff stared at him.

'What's going on?' said Geoff.

'Nothing,' said Brad. And he grinned at Geoff. 'Yet.'

The excitement over, P.J. and Winston and Speedy went up to the radio room with the map. They were going to plot the furthest they knew that Radio Rocket could reach and then they were going to put up posters. As P.J. pointed out, it wouldn't be much use broadcasting if they had no listeners.

Debbie Dobson saw them go. She was tired of playing table tennis. She was nosey too, and if she had ever seen anyone with a secret it was those three lads. So she gave them a bit of a start and then crept up the stairs after them.

Getting to the top of the stairs, she found herself in a part of the Grove where she hadn't been before. She hesitated a moment, then turned the corner into a very long corridor. As she walked along on tiptoe, listening for the lads' voices, she kept having a nagging sort of I-have-been-here-before feeling. Suddenly she thought she heard a noise behind her and whirled round sharply but there was nothing there. Then she stood stock still, not hearing anything except the beating of her own heart. The corridor seemed to stretch for miles behind her and, when she turned round again, it seemed to stretch even further in front. She thought she'd go back downstairs when at the very far end of the passage she saw a door opening slowly. The slit of light grew wider and, with a thrill of horror, she realised what the corridor reminded her of. It was exactly the same as the one in the film with the finger knife man. The hairs on the back of her neck prickled as she heard the sound she most dreaded in all the world. The snick, snick, snick of the sharp finger knives rubbing together. Giving an almighty shriek, she turned and ran for her life.

Behind the door, Winston was almost in hysterics as he

rubbed his nailfile against Speedy's penknife. Speedy was not so sure.

'What are you going to do if she runs straight to Geoff?' he demanded.

Winston shook his head. 'She'll never stop running till she gets home, man,' he said. 'Did you not hear her squeak? She'll be under the bedclothes for days.'

It was getting dark outside and the bushes down the track to the road were full of monsters as Debbie ran for her life, each rustle making her run faster and her heartbeat drumming in her ears till she finally came home and ran into the front gate in her panic. She wrestled it open and hammered on the front door.

The house was silent, its windows like red eyes reflecting the setting sun. Nobody was home. Debbie reached into the letter box, pulled up the key on the string and opened the door. She put all the lights on and shouted for her mother. No reply. When she got to the kitchen, there was a note on the kitchen table. Jemma had been sick and they had taken her to the doctor.

While she was reading the note, she stiffened suddenly, hearing a noise which didn't seem to belong to the house. She listened again but it had stopped. And then it started again, a sort of scuffling noise coming from the hall. She gathered all her courage together and opened the hall door. Through the frosted glass of the front door, she could see the shadow of a hunched figure, wearing the broad-brimmed hat of her nightmare! And, as she watched, the letter box opened and the dangling key was whisked up and out of sight. She sagged against the door, unable to move or utter anything more than a little squeak as the door opened slowly. Her heart pounded and pounded and seemed to lunge up her throat and fill her mouth. The door finally stood wide open and the figure in the hat looked at her.

'Debbie, pet,' said Gran. 'What in the world are you doing pressed up against the door for goodness sake?'

With a sob of relief, Debbie flew down the corridor and into Mary O'Malley's arms. And Gran did what all good grannies do. She listened to what ailed her little treasure and she made a silent vow to herself that somebody would get what was coming to them.

Fraser was cycling aimlessly along the same track Debbie had just flown down. He stopped his bike when he saw Duncan, wanting to ask if the little lad had seen Spuggie. But something in his manner made Fraser stop and he watched while that big yob, Carl, who was always hanging round Gill's squat slid out of the undergrowth. They seemed to be arguing and Fraser raised his voice.

'Duncan!' he called. Carl looked round, poked Duncan in the chest and swung himself over the wall like an ape. Fraser cycled up to Duncan.

'What are you doing with that guy?' asked Fraser. He liked Duncan and he didn't like the look of what he had just seen. 'He's poison, him.' But Duncan's reaction surprised him. It was jerky and hostile. 'Why don't you just mind your own business?' said Duncan. Fraser was persistent, in his own quiet way, and wouldn't be put off.

'If he's bullying you, all you've got to do is tell someone.'

Duncan snapped back that he could handle it and Fraser shrugged his shoulders. He supposed it was none of his business, and he had enough on his plate anyway with Spuggie's mysterious disappearances. Duncan told him he hadn't seen Spuggie and watched Fraser go.

He fingered the building society cash card in his pocket. He had to get some money from somewhere or else he was in big trouble with Carl. And Carl was too vicious to mess around with. He bit his lip and thought hard. The nearest cashpoint was miles away from Benwell but there was nothing else for it. He walked off, head down. Carl watched him from the bushes and grinned to himself. This was definitely the way to spin your giro out. Pity more kids didn't have Duncan's bad habits and need to borrow at the market rate. Which, in Carl's case, would have put the Mafia to shame.

Spuggie, in the meantime, had finally, reluctantly stopped learning to play chess and gone off to make Beckett's phone call. This time she was lucky and spoke to the man, who wasn't at all worried about getting a message from a young girl. He just repeated what she told him and said he'd pick Beckett up the next day. He couldn't say what time but Spuggie didn't think it would matter. Beckett wasn't going anywhere. Then she went off to do the second bit of the message. She was headed for the same cash machine as Duncan, with Beckett's number written on her hand in biro and his card tucked into the top of her knickers.

Geoff was having a bit of a culture shock. He'd found out what karaoke was, he'd found out how much a backing track of 'Jimmy Mac' would cost, and he was trying to find a way of telling Charlie and Hayley that there wasn't enough money in the kitty. When up popped Dexter to make a telephone call to a mate of his. He put the phone down and turned to Geoff with triumph written all over his face.

'What?' asked Geoff. And Dexter grinned and said he'd bring a tape in the next day. Geoff looked thoughtful. He didn't want to get up Dexter's nose. But equally he didn't want Dexter getting into the habit of doing favours for young female clients at the Grove. One thing led to another, in Geoff's experience. To his credit, Dexter could see Geoff's point and said so. He also promised to bring the tape in the next day. And he went, with a song in his heart.

Geoff breathed a sigh of relief. A premature sigh of relief, as a matter of fact, because Dexter had gone to look for Charlie to tell her the good news. After watching her and Hayley perform a finger-snapping, hip-swinging version of the song in question, backed by the one and only Byker

Grove male formation jive team, still consisting of P.J., Speedy and Winston and still looking like a bunch of fleas on a hotplate, Dexter siphoned Charlie off to one side. He told her the good news about the backing track and also told her where he was picking it up and when. Then he invited her down to the club herself, which left her pretty face in a cloud of indecision. Dexter did the smart thing and left her to think it over, promising that he wasn't going to make any moves and that everything was absolutely above board.

Meanwhile, Spuggie had got the money and was astonished to see Duncan arrive at the same machine. She looked at him suspiciously, convinced he was following her.

'What are you doing here?' she said, hiding the money quickly.

'I'm minding me own business,' said Duncan. 'You wanna try it, it's great.' And he stood and looked at her till she tossed her head and marched off back to the allotment.

Duncan's vice was playing arcade machines and it was eating every penny he had. First it took his paper delivery money, then the money from his gran which was in the building society and then the money from Geoff's cash box, after he had found the spare keys. He fingered the card in his pocket, wedged it quickly in the machine and punched the keypad before he could change his mind. He had to pay Carl back. But he had to have some money to play the games too.

Spuggie bounced along towards the allotment. She was deep in thought, hugging the secret of Beckett deep inside her, when the sudden, brazen howling of a police car jerked her back to real life. She didn't connect it with Beckett until she got to the allotment and saw that the place was swarming with policemen. She watched with dread, the barking dogs and the chatter of the police radios making a nasty background music to her thoughts. The hut door was open. There was no sign of Beckett, though, and she began to hope again. She walked slowly past the allotment and towards the big thicket of trees on the other side of the road. There was a bus stop in front of it where a couple of women were standing, wagging their heads at the fuss. Then she saw Beckett ease his way over the wall and edge closer to the bus stop. One of the women turned and gave him a sharp glance. Spuggie stood stock still. Then she called out in a loud, clear voice and ran across the road to place her hand trustingly inside Beckett's.

'Dad!' she scolded. 'Where have you been?' I've been stood over there for ages.' And she looked towards the allotment. 'What's going on over there?'

Beckett looked down at her and she could see the fine drops of sweat on his forehead. He managed a faint smile. But the women had forgotten about him by now and then the bus came and they both got on it. Spuggie took him to the block of flats and hid him in the little place at the back of the stairs. It was smelly but it would do until she could think of something else.

Charlie couldn't eat her tea. She fidgeted and fussed until she could decently get up and leave. Her mother looked at her with resignation.

'Where are you going?' she asked eventually. 'Haven't you got any homework?'

'We had a free period,' said Charlie.

'You'll miss *Top of the Pops*,' her mother said.

Charlie rolled her eyes. 'Mother! Please!' she went up to her room to look at herself. To be exact, she went to look at the spot which threatened to turn into a life-wrecking carbuncle. She wondered whether to squeeze but settled for some green stuff which took the red out of it and her tightest shortest skirt which she hoped would keep eyes off it. She was down the stairs and out of the house before her mother could complain about the skirt.

And then it was the Metro and a swift walk through some

very dark streets until she came to the club where Dexter had said to come.

He was there all right, large as life and in a leather jacket and tight jeans which made him look less ordinary and a bit more, well, dangerous. He pressed a button and the iron security door rolled up like the door to a new life. She hesitated.

'Come on,' said Dexter. 'It's fine. Trust me!'

And she went down the long corridor to a door at the end, behind which she could hear the deep, rhythmic beat of a bass line.

And Dexter followed, grinning to himself.

CHAPTER THREE

Spuggie thought hard as she raced up the stairs – the lifts were still out of order. She rushed into the flat where Fraser was waiting, his face stern.

'Where have you been?' he demanded. Then he looked at her closely.

'You've got cobwebs in your hair. How d'you get cobwebs in your hair?'

Spuggie really needed some help and Fraser was the only one she could trust. But before she could ask him, her mother came in, blinking at the light. Her face was haunted. She looked at the clock.

'Isn't your dad back yet? Man, it's late. Where's he got to, this hour of the night?'

Neither of the children had seen their father since the night he'd stormed out in a rage, more than a month ago. Fraser took his mother gently by the arm, told Spuggie to get a cup of tea and gently led Betty Campbell to bed. She protested as she went out.

'I've got to get your dad's tea. You know what he's like if his tea's not on the table.'

Fraser reassured her, and she went with him, not really aware of what was happening. Fraser took his time, smoothing the bed and helping her into it. She returned to reality briefly as she looked at him.

'Man, Fraser, you've grown.'

He nodded, fighting to swallow the lump in his throat, and offered her the headache pills. She shook her head but then caught his arm, brightening.

'You can bring us that bottle of tonic wine, pet. That might perk us up a bit.'

'It's broke, Mam,' he said. She looked sly and knowing at the same time and shook her head again.

'There's another one at the back of the airing cupboard,'

she told him. 'I have to hide it,' she went on. 'I don't want Kirstie thinking it's pop. If she drank that, it'd make her ill.'

He took a deep breath and went to fetch it. But before he took the bottle back in, he poured half the wine down the sink. The sickly sweet smell made him gag, as he refilled the bottle with water.

Having left the wine bottle by the side of the bed, he made himself some toast and beans from the stack of food Spuggie had brought. As he ate, he thought about what to do next. They would have to get the doctor, of course. But getting the doctor meant a visit from the social worker too and that would mean some careful lying if he and his sister were to avoid being taken into care.

Meanwhile, Spuggie had darted downstairs to move Beckett while it was dark. As for Beckett, he knew that his position was getting more insecure by the minute. He should really have taken the bull by the horns when he had the chance and tried for a lift out of town at one of the transport cafes. But motorways made such places harder to find and harder still to get to from the centres of big towns. So he followed the red hair of his little will-o'-the-wisp, knowing that he was becoming more attached to Spuggie by the minute and if he was honest he was staying in Newcastle more to watch over her than to save his own skin. Just give it another day, he thought. And then go.

She took him down the byways of the hill above the town, spread out with twinkling lights as the dark began to bite. Then she took him over the wall of the Grove and they hid in the bushes by the leek trench until they heard Geoff and Mary O'Malley locking up and saying goodnight. Finally she took him into the cellar where she had chased the cat. Climbing through the window, he slipped, landing heavily and jarring his angle. Spuggie heard the muffled cursing.

'Are you all right?' she asked anxiously, through the window.

'I am,' he said, testing the ankle but having to sit down with the pain. 'You go home. We'll see to it tomorrow.'

They agreed that she would get some bandages for the morning. Then she went and Beckett settled back with his thoughts. The little animal rustles and scuffles didn't bother him. He went to sleep eventually and dreamed of a little girl with red hair who might have been his daughter.

Over at the Riverfront Club, after Charlie had got over the shock of finding Hayley already there, she had another shock. Dexter did know a man who ran an independent record company. And he wanted to hear them sing then and there. This nearly sent Charlie straight into freefall. But Hayley jollied her along until it started to seem like a very good idea and the two kids strutted their stuff, innocently and provocatively all at the same time, Charlie dressed in patterned tights and short black shirt, blonde hair flashing and swinging, Hayley with a wicked set of gear that was nearly as wicked as her eyes.

Steve Rettega watched and drew on a cigarette and Dexter watched Rettega watch. Dexter wasn't as bad as he liked people to think. He'd seen talent, in Charlie particularly, and he wanted to help.

'I told you,' said Dexter.

'Aye, you did,' replied Rettega. 'How old are they?'

Dexter shrugged and Rettega nodded to himself. As young as that, he thought, and put his cigarette away. The record had stopped and the two girls were little girls again, giggling together and shooting coy glances his way. Rettega couldn't get the little French girl out of his mind, the one who'd made a major killing a couple of years before. Vanessa Paradis that was the name, with 'Joe le Taxi'. And Kylie herself didn't look old enough to be out on her own. He smiled at them and made it as nice a smile as he could. They grinned back. And Steve told them the good news. Which made their heads spin, and sent them rushing off to the hub of Newcastle teenage nightlife.

At the Metro Centre, the lights were on and the crowd was moving and the pirate radio magnates were discussing very important programming details. They didn't have all that many records, that was the main problem. And they couldn't think straight, as they were rocking with laughter at Winston's latest wheeze. Winston thought they needed an agony aunt and, after all the jokes about Oprah Wincey, he'd suggested Kelly. Robert shook his head gravely.

'There's three kinds of communication in this world, Winston. Telephone, telegram and tell a woman. Tell Kelly about this and she'll have it all over Byker Grove within minutes.'

Winston shook his head angrily and stuck to his guns. Then he produced the clincher. 'Let her do it,' he said. 'And I'll definitely borrow me dad's mobile phone.'

The other lads looked at each other. Speedy was doubtful. 'You said that yesterday,' he pointed out.

But Winston talked louder and louder and faster and faster and finally convinced them all, except Speedy.

'This'll end in tears,' he prophesied darkly. One of Speedy's specialities was sounding like an elderly aunt and P.J. looked at him and pursed his lips. 'Only if you start crying,' he said and they were all laughing again. Robert felt his face flush suddenly as he saw Charlie weaving through the tables with Hayley. There were bright spots of pink on her cheeks and her eyes were enchanted. The two girls came up to the table, Charlie looked at Robert and he hoped that nobody else would understand the way they were gazing at each other. His voice came out gruff.

'What's eating you two?' he croaked and could have died on the spot. But she was too excited to notice his embarrassment.

'It's a secret,' she said but promised silently to tell him

everything. He couldn't stop himself giving her a little grin and Speedy looked cross. He could see that Charlie was going to be a major problem, thrusting herself on Robert like this. Girls!

'If I don't tell someone, I'll burst,' said Hayley and hopped from foot to foot with excitement. Speedy nodded.

'Telephone!' he said and the others took it up. 'Telegram!' said Winston. And 'Tell a woman!' P.J. finished. But Charlie and Robert didn't care. They just looked at each other. Robert had never seen anything as beautiful as her. To his horror he felt his cheeks growing pink again and had to drop back into his gruff mode.

'Women can't keep secrets,' he said.

'It's a scientific fact,' Speedy added, nodding, but Hayley and Charlie weren't impressed.

'Is it?' said Hayley and Charlie added, 'Right! Now you'll never know,' and they both danced off, tossing their heads. Speedy looked at Robert and cursed inwardly as he clocked the silly grin.

The next day at the Grove, there was a little crisis which quickly grew into a much bigger, more serious crisis. Alan Dobson came down with Jemma, his youngest, and Debbie the middle sister. It would have been the full set except that Nicola was still at Scarborough with Donna and her dad and Lisa. He looked at the leeks and shook his head as he prodded the soil. They were further on than they should have been and he told Geoff so. Then he looked at Geoff and it was clear that there was something else bothering him.

'What's up? asked Geoff and Alan shook his head.

'If I tell you, I'm more than likely to lose me temper.' And his normally good natured face was very taut. 'Have a word with our Debbie, will you?' he said.

Debbie didn't want to say anything at first. She sat in Geoff's office and her eyes were big and her face was scared and her mouth was stubborn. 'They told us to keep me mouth shut,' she said and looked pleadingly at her granny. But this was what Geoff was good at and he questioned her gently, with humour and patience, and eventually got the whole sorry tale out of her. And when she'd finished, she burst out crying with relief.

'That's all right, pet,' he said, patting her reassuringly.

Then he walked into the entrance hall, right into the bunch of lads he was looking for. They'd been out flyposting and were laughing themselves sick. The highlight had been flyposting a police car without PC Grant seeing them and they were still hammering each other on the back with glee. When they saw Geoff's face the mood changed at once. They stopped laughing and tried to slide past but Geoff wasn't having any of that. He jerked a thumb at the door.

'My office,' he said. 'Now!' They looked at each other.

'What's up, Geoff?' P.J. ventured.

Geoff turned. 'We're just going to have a word about some impromptu video sessions,' he said. They looked at each other again. 'And about scaring little girls like Debbie Dobson and thinking it's funny.' They started to give their reasons and excuses but he shut them all up with a look and they filed mutinously into his office where they stood in a ring with their heads down. Except for Robert who sat in the ring. But Robert's head was down too.

And then Geoff nearly blasted them into orbit. What they'd done was simple enough. They'd got a horror film out and they'd enjoyed watching it. They'd also let Debbie watch it and it had given her nightmares. Which confirmed the 'Tell a woman' theory in all their minds.

'I obviously made the mistake of assuming you were all grown up,' said Geoff, surveying the hangdog looks but not being fooled by them. With a young lad, a hangdog look and a quick apology often cuts a punishment down. Every young lad had that look ready.

Robert felt obliged to fight back. 'That's not fair, Geoff,' he said in his best let's-all-be-men-together voice. His voice was just about to break and was in its darkest brown phase at the moment. It wasn't consistent though, and let him down this time by squeaking on the last syllable.

Geoff's reply was short and to the point. How fair was it to give a thirteen-year-old child nightmares? Silence might have finished the interview there, but P.J., Robert and Speedy cursed inwardly as they heard Winston draw breath.

'Nobody made her watch,' said Winston. Strictly speaking, this was true, but, more importantly, it gave Geoff the perfect opening.

'Stupid remark, Winston,' he said and even Winston could see he was right. Geoff continued into the silence. 'The video recorder's out of bounds to everybody for the next month. I'm locking it away.' They filed out in that peculiarly resentful way which naughty lads have when they've been found out. It's not fair, said every inch of their backs and the back of their necks and Geoff grinned a little to himself.

When he looked up, they'd gone and in their place stood Medallion Man. It was Steve Rettega, complete with leather jacket, gold chain, tight trousers, greasy smile and cocky manner. Geoff looked once and then looked again. Rettega's smile seemed to say that he knew he looked like a prat but invited you to sympathise with him for having to turn out in public looking the way he did. Geoff waited, determined not to judge him too harshly right from the start. Find out what he's got to say first, then you can dislike him with a clear conscience. Rettega smiled. Geoff changed his mind and started to dislike him right away. Apart from the fact that he was older and thinner than Geoff, he had better teeth.

'You must be Geoff,' said Steve.

Geoff nodded. 'Aye,' he said, not giving anything away. He might be Geoff but there was nothing that said he had to be.

'And who might you be?' he asked. Rettega handed him a business card, black and shiny and covered with gold letters and musical notes. Geoff read the name and handed it back, unimpressed. 'So?' he said. 'Polythene Records. Mr Rettega. What can I do for you?'

'Call me Steve,' said Rettega. 'Maybe,' said Geoff, 'when I get to know you a bit better. Now, what can I do for you?'

Rettega nodded and smiled. He was used to being welcomed with less than open arms. 'I met a couple of your more charming clients last night,' he said.

Geoff waited.

Rettega assumed an air of innocence. 'Your man, Dexter,' he said, 'brought them down to the Riverfront Club.' He smiled. 'I assume that was with your permission?'

Geoff's face was taut again. 'Not exactly,' he said.

Rettega was a little perturbed. 'I hope I haven't got him into trouble at all,' he said. Actually he didn't care how much trouble he'd managed to get Dexter in. But he did want to get Dexter away from the girls. Dexter was an unknown quantity. And when you're dealing with talented little girls and their parents, the last thing you want hanging around is an unknown quantity. Especially one with tight jeans and an attitude problem.

Geoff heaved a big sigh and waved at the chair. Rettega sat down. 'So,' said Geoff. 'What's it all about, Mr Rettega? Might as well clear it up before I sack the little squit.'

'It won't come to that, surely,' said Rettega. Geoff looked up sharply and Rettega smiled. 'Sorry,' he said quickly.

'Aye,' said Geoff. 'I'm not that green. You told me what you just told me because you wanted me to do something about Dexter.' Rettega nodded.

'So what's your interest in the two girls. I assume it *is* Hayley and Charlie, isn't it?' And Steve Rettega settled himself in his chair and set about winning the heart and mind of the man who ran Byker Grove. Because he wouldn't get very far with the parents if Geoff wasn't on his side.

And deep in the bowels of Byker Grove, Beckett tried to ignore the pain in his throbbing ankle as Spuggie practised her first aid, making him wince every now and then. She finished and gave the ankle a trial pat, watching Beckett's face as she did so. He managed to keep his face straight but he didn't fool Spuggie.

'You've not to be hopping round on that, you know,' she said, her face stern. He managed not to smile but that didn't fool her either. 'And it's nothing to laugh about,' she said firmly. 'You might have to do some running when your friend comes. And I can't help you out through the window. You'll be on your own.' He nodded.

They'd agreed that she would make one more telephone call and that would be the end of it. She wanted desperately to ask him if there was any chance that she might be able to come with him but at the last minute her courage failed her and she just scraped her way out through the window, tearing her jeans and getting dirt all over her knees. She made her way round to the front of the Grove as if she had just arrived and, just her luck, ran straight into Gwen, eyes shining behind her glasses, glad to be back from her course, full of goodwill and nosiness. Spuggie looked right through her but it didn't work.

'Hello, Spuggie,' said Gwen. 'And how are you today?' Spuggie just grunted and walked straight past. Geoff saw the exchange as he came out of his office, carrying the video recorder.

'I hope you're going to try and put things right with Spuggie, Gwen,' he said. She turned, looking puzzled, not knowing what he meant.

'Sorry?' she said. And he stopped and looked at her. 'I hope, you're going to use what you learned on that course to make things right with Spuggie. Or have I wasted another huge portion of a tiny budget?'

She flushed. 'There's no need to be like that, Geoff,' she answered. But he had already gone on this way to lock the video machine in the cellar. He was still seething with what Rettega had told him and there was no way to deal with it until Dexter came back from the Town Hall where he had been for a career interview. Not that he would have any career left at Byker Grove if Geoff had anything to do with it. He unlocked the door to the cellar and looked down. It was dark and dusty inside and Geoff didn't feel like dirtying yet another pair of trousers in the service of Newcastle youth. So he just put the machine down on the top step, came out and locked the door behind him. It would be as safe there as anywhere. And Beckett was left with his teeth gritted and his heart jumping in alarm in the dark and the dust.

Gwen was still feeling stung by Geoff's reaction and made her way to Spuggie to try again. She called her over. Spuggie turned but her deliberately blank expression gave Gwen no encouragement. She walked across to Spuggie, feeling a little cross. It was really silly of the child to make so much fuss about not getting the vet's assistant's job. In fact, it was her own fault. If Spuggie had said how old she was in the first place, they would have known she was too young and she wouldn't have even been considered and all this awkwardness would have been avoided. Gwen's life, for the most part, did consist of avoiding awkwardness. She flushed a little, remembering the course she had just finished and the very rude man from Stoke who had accused her of being the 'anything for a quiet life' type of leader. Summoning a little smile, she looked at the red-haired mite who was causing her all the trouble.

'Can I have a word?' said Gwen, 'In private?'

Spuggie shook her head. 'I've got to go home,' she said. 'Me mam's not well.'

Gwen seized the opportunity. 'I'll give you a lift,' she said. 'I really would like to talk to you.' And Spuggie couldn't get out of it.

When Fraser came in a bit later, looking for Spuggie, he was annoyed to find out what had happened. He pedalled off. There really would be sand in the vaseline if nosey

67

Gwen managed to get inside the Campbell flat and found out about Betty Campbell. As he went down the drive, he passed Gill, long-time stranger coming up the drive in his grease-stained overalls. Gill's face broke into a smile but Fraser was gone with a brief shout, leaving his friend to walk up to the door of the Grove. Which was somewhere he'd grown out of, but which had fond memories for him. Also, someone might know where Julie was. He hadn't seen her for ages and every time he rang her house, her rotten father answered and put the phone down as soon as he found out it was Gill.

Charlie and Haley were idly practising dance steps and singing 'Jimmy Mac' as he came close. Charlie flirted a little with her eyes and Hayley nudged her. 'Hey, you!' whispered Hayley. 'One at a time! You've already got that cripple lad's wheel bearings smoking.'

Charlie turned on Hayley. 'He's not a cripple,' she said angrily but Gill came right up to them, stopping any retort from Hayley.

She, in turn, gave him her warmest smile, getting a nudge from Charlie for her pains. 'Hi, Gill,' she said. 'Looking for Julie?'

He nodded dourly. 'Aye, I was,' he said. 'I was.'

Hayley pulled a face. 'Since her mam left home, she's having trouble with her dad. He's trying to ground her, I think.' Gill nodded and mooched off. This was no more than he'd expected.

The two girls watched him go. They knew they'd been in the presence of true love in a bind and they spoke in hushed voices. Charlie was the first to break the silence. 'He's lovely, isn't he?' she said longingly. Hayley looked at her and burst out giggling.

'What?' said Charlie indignantly and then giggled herself.

'Did they not have boys at Denton Burn then?' said Hayley. 'You talk as if you'd been on a desert island for ten years, you do!'

Charlie smiled but Hayley wasn't all that far from the truth. Going out with Greg had been very like living on a desert island for all the boys she'd been allowed to talk to. But things were changing. She hugged herself. There was Robert and there was the chance of making a record. And her eyes glowed. Things were definitely changing.

Meanwhile, Fraser got to the block of flats and groaned silently. He could see Gwen's mouth going nineteen to the dozen, while Spuggie sat in the front seat, not saying anything. He rode up and banged on the glass. Spuggie rolled her widow down and he spoke before Gwen could get a word in.

'Come on, Spuggie,' he said. 'Where have you been? Mam's got the tea ready,' They both went inside and Gwen sat in the car, convinced that something was wrong but not sure what. Finally she started up the engine and drove away.

After Gill had mooched off from the Grove, he'd found he could either get the bus home or have chips for his tea. Not fish and chips, mind, just chips. And that meant he wasn't exactly in the best of tempers when he got home and found Carl sat reading in the derelict car behind the squat, with the obscene-looking sexless shop mannequin next to him. They didn't speak but Gill could feel Carl's eyes on his back as he went up the steps, then up the stairs and into the room which he now called home. He put the light on and the bulb burst with a pop, sending him into an even blacker mood. He tossed the packet of chips on the settee and sat down.

Looking round the room, in spite of his sour mood, maybe even because of it, he grinned ruefully. A couple of months ago, this would have been mega. A place of his own, nobody to bother him, money in his pocket at least some of the time. Now all he could see were the mouldy patches on the wall and, if he looked hard enough, the mouldy patches in his life. He couldn't think any further than Julie and longed for the feel of her smooth, cool face on his, her soft lips, tender and demanding at the same time, the little curl of her eyelashes against his cheek, the way she looked at him, half committed and in love and half teasing, mocking, driving him crazy. He looked at his big, bony hands with the muck under the fingernails and the oil and grease under the skin of his palms. A fat lot he had to offer Julie Warner, a garage labourer with a feel for mending high-speed sports cars and never a chance of earning enough to buy one. No wonder her father always put the phone down.

He poked in his chip packet but they'd gone cold and disgusting. He thought of who he could borrow a pound off till the next day, maybe a fiver, a tenner even, get himself totally out of the game, smash a few snakebites down him, do himself the world of bad. Then if he had a headache, he'd have an excuse to go with it. He hurled himself out of the door and clattered down the stairs and the steps, bent on teaching himself a lesson. Watched sardonically by Carl, he ran down the alley and collided with a soft and yielding body. There was a little silence and he looked deep into Julie's eyes.

'Hello, stranger,' she said and smiled at him. His guts did a backflip and all he could do was answer feebly, trying to stay cool.

'Hi!,' he said and paused while he struggled to think of something to say that would keep her there with him. 'I thought you were grounded,' he said.

'You know what thought did?' she answered pertly and a mounting tide of alarm and excitement swept through him. Something had changed. She'd changed, he didn't know how but it was going to be all right! He knew it!

'Aren't you going to invite me back to your place?' she smiled, and he took his time, hardly daring to answer for fear of what he might hear.

'Why should I?' he joked at last.

And she held his eyes with her own and he couldn't, didn't want to, look away. And she breathed the next words, almost

70

shyly but with all the purpose and determination in the world. 'Because,' Julie said. 'Because I want to come and live with you.'

He put his arm round her waist and walked her back to his place. And this time nothing mattered. Not the car, not the hairless mannequin, not Carl's piggy eyes. They were together again, for real. And this time they were going to stay together.

CHAPTER FOUR

Sometimes people look at Geoff and his potbelly and his slightly out-of-date moustache and what they see is very close to a figure of fun. What they don't see is the fierce dedication and pride Geoff brings to his job. An outsider might make the same sort of mistake about the Grove.

Byker Grove is not just a youth club. It's not a youth club at all, to tell you the truth. If you ask Geoff what it is, all you'll probably get is some kind of corny Geordie joke and then he'll go and do something a long way off round the back in case anyone else wants to ask any stupid questions. Put simply, Byker Grove is a place where young people can come and learn how to grow up. Somewhere where even if they do make the odd mistake, it's not a disaster and a cup of Mary's tea and a laugh with your mates can go a long way towards mending anything, from a broken heart to a tyre puncture or a hidden worry that grows a lot smaller when you take it out and look at it.

All the kids who go to the Grove are Geoff's sacred charges. Nothing bad will happen to them, nothing in the whole wide world, if Geoff has anything to do with it. Geoff's in love with the Grove. He's also in love with all the kids that go there although, like many love affairs, there's always the chance that this one may end in tears.

No wonder Geoff really wound his clock about the news that Rettega brought him and Dexter's part in it. Of course Dexter had invited Charlie and Hayley down to the club without asking or telling Geoff. He'd done this for a very good reason. He knew damn well that Geoff would never have let them go.

Dexter was in very good heart as he ran up the path to the Grove. To be fair to him, he really didn't have any designs on Charlie or Hayley when he invited them up to the club. Rettega's company had been looking for someone to out-Kylie Kylie Minogue and when Rettega had heard that his old drinking buddy Dexter would be working at a youth club, he'd said to keep an eye out for some chubby pink local talent with a voice.

And that was how it had started, right enough. Except that when Charlie had marched into the club and Rettega had clocked Dexter, whose tongue was nearly cleaning his shoes, he had realised that a fifteen-year-old in bobby sox and box-fresh trainers was a vastly different proposition to one in patterned black tights, a skirt that would have made a respectable cake frill and high heels. So as soon as he knew she could sing, he did the right thing. The right thing for Rettega even though it meant dropping Dexter neck deep in manure. He went down to the Grove, all innocence, marked Geoff's card and made sure that Dexter was off the strength. He also rang Mr and Mrs Charlton and told them the good news which was that he would try to groom their talented little daughter into a pop star. He also let his wife ring them to prove that there would be a chaperone along all the time.

Now, seeing Dexter running up the drive, Geoff leaned out of his office to call Gwen. She looked puzzled.

'I want you with me when I talk to Dexter,' he explained.

'Why?' said Gwen. 'What's up?'

Geoff's face reflected his thoughts. 'I need someone with me,' he told her, 'to keep me from strangling the little scut.'

The interview was short and nasty and Dexter mouthed off as much as he could after Geoff sacked him for taking little girls out to a nightclub.

'Steve Rettega's going to give them a chance,' he protested. 'That's all I took them down there for.'

Geoff shook his head. 'He's the one that complained,' he said and Dexter knew then that he'd been sold down the river. He also thought he knew why Steve had done it. So Dexter couldn't claim any of the credit for discovering Charlie and Hayley. He looked at Geoff and, as so often before, his nasty side burst out.

'Aye, right,' he said. 'Well, it makes no difference. I can wait. The blonde'll be sixteen in a couple of months. Then she can make up her own mind.' And he braced his back and his shoulders. Gwen drew in her breath sharply.

When Geoff spoke, his tone was measured and his voice quiet. 'If you want your teeth to go with you, Dexter,' he said, 'you'll go now. And if I see you within a mile of Byker Grove the same will apply. Day or night.' Dexter stood his ground for no more than a moment. Then he ducked his head quickly, turned and went. Gwen looked at Geoff fearfully. This was a Geoff she had not seen before.

While she watched, the old Geoff came back and gave her a quick, rueful grin from under the big, bushy moustache. 'Sorry,' he said. She shook her head to show that it didn't matter and he went on to tell her that, provided the Grove could send someone down to the studios with Hayley and Charlie, there would be no difficulty with either set of parents. Gwen agreed, glad to see the back of the nasty moment she had just witnessed. It wasn't till a few minutes later that she realised she'd also agreed to be chaperone. Which was a bit unlucky, really, because Gwen's knowledge of pop music began and ended with James Last. In fact what Gwen knew about pop you could have written down on a hen's beak. But this was handy, Geoff pointed out, because it meant she wouldn't be blinded by the glamour of showbiz. She nodded glumly. At least she could take a book.

And so she did. She took the Rachel Carson book about how the world was being polluted by all its inhabitants and as Hayley and Charlie sang with vigour, she reflected on the title, *The Silent Spring*. Fat chance!

Steve Rettega was as good as his word and gave the project the whole of his attention. The studio was all set up and the girls sang their way through quite a few numbers, while he handled the tracks and a morose technician did the mixing. Steve nodded to himself as he watched Charlie throw her head back and let all the joy and hope that was in her flood out through her throat. The other kid, Hayley, was OK too but she was a little more predictable, a little more knowing. Charlie was pure gold and Steve had seen enough brass to know the difference.

The session ended and Rettega loaded them all in his car to take them home. On the way, they stopped to fill up with fizzy drinks and burgers which was Gwen's cue to tell them all about how beef farming was destroying the rainforests. She did this with one eye on Rettega, waiting for a snide comment. He was a lot brighter than that, though. He was sober and sensible and charming, and agreed with her entirely. She didn't know, of course, that one of the first rules in Steve's business was never to make an enemy by accident and having Gwen on his side was very much part of his plans for Charlie. As Steve thought this, he watched Charlie's face, full of the innocence and fun he'd once had himself. She caught him looking at her and something in his eyes made her stop and look at him more carefully.

'What's the matter?' she said anxiously. 'Aren't we any good?'

He smiled a little. Then he told them what he planned. A solo single for one of them, he hadn't made his mind up properly yet and it would depend on finding the right song. Hayley and Charlie looked at each other and then back at him. And then a duet, Bananarama-type stuff. He grinned as they winced and then he set their minds at rest. The song he wanted them to do was 'Jimmy Mac'. They were good at it and it would go down well. The warm, friendly grins grew bigger and bigger and it was four very happy people who finally said goodbye to each other that evening.

Life was going on much as usual at the Grove while all this was happening. The four musketeers were practising being rock and roll tycoons and all the conversation was totally obscure to anyone not in on the secret. Also, they'd wedged the door of the radio room shut so nobody could get in anyway. After the first flush of enthusiasm, Winston's ambition had faded a little. He was beginning to regret having pushed Kelly's claims to be the agony aunt. Apart from anything else, he hadn't actually asked her if she wanted to do it. But the major problem had to do with his father's mobile telephone which he'd promised to borrow. He had about as much chance of getting it as Newcastle United had of winning *Come Dancing*. And then there was the leeks. Winston had decided that they were going to win the competition and, being Winston, had also decided to leave as little as possible to chance. He was thinking of running a book on the event and he was looking to influence the odds in his favour. He approached the leek bed with a scheme in his head and a large bottle of all-purpose plant fertiliser under his jacket. He looked around. There was nobody about and he bent down to feed the leeks a little. Behind him, Kelly's voice made him leap in the air, rather like the frog Spuggie had been so entranced by.

'What are you doing?' said Kelly and Winston turned to see her bright, friendly, suspicious eyes shining at him. Kelly liked Winston but that didn't mean she altogether trusted him. 'What have you got under your jacket?' she asked, poking a questing little hand around his ribs. Winston jumped and jerked.

'Get off!' he said, trying to get away. 'You're tickling!'

Speedy, Robert and P.J. clocked the intimate little scene and roared up, laughing and pushing each other.

'Look at this!' said Speedy. 'Love's young dream!' added Robert. And P.J. applied the final witty touch, 'Put him down, Kelly . . . You don't know where he's been.'

Winston finally managed to get loose. Kelly's face was flushed but she was enjoying herself. The boys' comments grew more pointed. 'If you don't want people to see you doing your courting,' said Speedy, 'do it in the bushes.'

'Aye,' said Robert. 'If you do it out in the open, you'll frighten all the horses.'

'Get off!' said Kelly, blushing for real this time but Speedy started to look around to see where the horses were. And by the time they'd sorted that one out and got to the real reason for the lads' coming down, she'd managed to get the red out of her cheeks. What they wanted was to run a trial with Kelly as the agony aunt to make sure she didn't dry up when she was really on air.

She was secretly pleased, of course, if a little perturbed by the idea of doing it for real. But they soon talked her round, and off they went, with Winston managing to drop the fertiliser down behind a bush.

As soon as they were out of sight, Carl picked it up. Carl was a watcher and everything that happened interested him. What interested him most at that particular moment was what Duncan had told him about the video recorder. Apparently it was locked in the cellar because of some kids' games. In Carl's book, this was a waste of a valuable piece of equipment. He slipped the bottle of fertiliser into his pocket and stalked round to the back of the Grove. Maybe there was another way in?

He was just in time to see a flash of red hair as Spuggie skidded round the corner. He waited a moment, started to follow, then stopped, puzzled. Behind the building there was a sort of square area, covered with weeds and odd bits of rubbish. But there was no Spuggie and she couldn't possibly have got right across the back yard in the short time she'd been out of sight. He started to move closer but was startled by voices and swung himself over the wall just as Brad and a council workman went by.

Spuggie was in the cellar, of course, with Beckett. She sat, satisfied, and watched him munch his way through a Cornish pasty, the first of several, to be washed down with chocolate flavoured milk. He grinned at her but she took her time about grinning back.

'You look tired,' she said at last. And he did. There were big black hollows under his eyes and the black beard was

77

starting to show very clearly through his white skin. He was beginning to look like a tramp, the sort the police would stop and question just because of the way he looked. He was wearing an old jacket he'd found in the corner of the allotment hut to keep him warm. If he didn't get away soon . . . She let the thought sink to the back of her mind. No use worrying about it. He got the chessboard out and they were soon absorbed in a game, black head bent close to flame hair.

Meanwhile, Geoff was talking to the council man about various maintenance problems. He was always having to defend the Grove against the planners. The latest problem was the lavatories which needed some money spending on them. Geoff was afraid that if too much money was needed, they might not do the work and then they might decide to shut the whole place down. He worked on the man and, in the end, they agreed to do what they could without exactly wasting any money on materials.

'If I could lock my tools up somewhere safe,' said Benny, the maintenance man, 'I could nip off this evening to do a bit. Then we wouldn't have any trouble with worksheets either.'

Geoff nodded, truly grateful, and opened the door to the cellar to show him where the tools could go. Then he stopped and listened. In the instant before he had opened the door and just after, he could have sworn he had heard something, voices or what, he didn't know. He bent his head sideways to hear better.

Down below, Spuggie and Beckett froze, hearing the door open. Beckett blew the candle out and they waited, hardly daring to breathe. The darkness was so black that Spuggie felt she could touch it. It pressed round her menacingly, and she felt comforted by Beckett's arm round her shoulders.

At the top of the steps, Geoff listened, watched by Benny. Then he shook his head. 'Ghosts!' he said. 'Place is full of them.' Then he saw Benny's face and laughed, taking him

78

away to reassure him. Which was just as well for Spuggie and Beckett.

Geoff had shut the door a moment before the acrid smell from the blown-out candle reached the top of the stairs. Beckett lit it again and they turned back to the chessboard. He smiled, seeing an opening, and taking Spuggie's bishop. 'I'm sorry about this,' he said. 'Chess is an unforgiving game.'

'Yes,' she agreed, 'check.' She smiled at him blandly as she took his queen. And they played on and as they played Beckett marvelled at her speed of thought. Her hand went over her mouth as she yawned. He looked at her, worried.

'You're not getting enough beauty sleep, yawning like that,' he said. 'Or am I boring?' She shook her head and told him about her mam not being well in the night. He looked concerned, and even more so when he found out that her father was away. Watching his face, she knew he understood that 'away' meant not coming back. He stretched his leg and winced. Now it was Spuggie's turn to be concerned.

'What's up with your foot?' she said. He shook his head to show that there was nothing wrong but she was too quick for him and rolled up his trouser leg to show how swollen his ankle was. What was worse, he'd cut himself too and the wound was angry red with yellow showing along the rim of the cut. Her heart leapt with fright. She put her hand on it.

'That's terrible,' she stammered. You'll have to get that looked at. It's all hot!'

Beckett knew she was right but he didn't know what to do about it. He needed a car out of here and he needed it quickly. Just one more phone call and a meeting place would do it. He put his hand out and touched her arm.

'OK,' he said soothingly. 'I'll be gone tomorrow. I'll get it fixed when I get to where I live.'

She was not convinced. 'How are you going to get out with a leg like that?' But he was thinking. 'Do they lock that gate at the end of the drive?' he asked. She shook her head.

'I'll write down what to say,' he told her and she shook her head again, saying she would remember.

'OK!' he said. 'Tell them to bring the car right round the back and tell them to bring a rope or something I can hang on to. Tell them I've hurt my foot and I'll need a bit of help, OK?' She nodded, very serious now, and scurried out through the window, off home to enlist Fraser's help.

Up in the radio room, things were hotting up. Robert had sadly accepted that he couldn't be there. He was too much of a hazard in case they had to make a quick getaway, so he rolled his wheelchair moodily off towards the leek bed. Kelly was on absolute pins. The rehearsal for the agony column had come to a spluttering halt. The questions the lads had invented had got sillier and sillier, and Kelly had ended up saying that if anyone came up with anything really rude, she'd just tell them to wash their mouths out and put the phone down. Then Fraser arrived and told them about his problem with the incredible disappearing sister. Kelly looked at him as if he was mad.

'Spuggie's here, man,' she said. 'I saw her climbing over the wall with a carrier bag just before.' Fraser shook his head. It was all getting a bit beyond him.

Then P.J. brought them all back to the matter in hand and, within minutes, they were on the air, first with one jingle and then the dulcet tones of P.J., making like a breakfast-time DJ.

The only people who heard the broadcast and didn't enjoy it were the crew of an ambulance who were trying to find a heart attack victim. The Radio Rocket transmission cut right through their wavelength, breaking up the message. The driver stopped and cursed and tried to retune. But it was no use. He banged his hand on the wheel in frustration and started looking for a telephone box.

Geoff was on the telephone himself at that moment, watched by Gwen and Mary O'Malley. Gwen was talking, mainly to try and lessen the tension.

'I like a string quartet myself so far as music is concerned.'

'Aye,' said Mary O'Malley, her anxious eyes fixed on Geoff. He was finally ringing the police to report the loss of money from the cash box.

Gwen went on. 'But I do quite like some of the sixties' protest songs. I honestly believe, for instance, that Dylan awakened the liberal pulse of the youth of the era.' She looked at Mary who was miles away, hoping that none of the kids had been stealing money.

'What?' said Mary.

'Dylan,' repeated Gwen. Mary looked puzzled.

'Wasn't he the rabbit in *The Magic Roundabout*?' Gwen shook her head sadly.

Geoff put the telephone down. 'Bob Grant's coming over as soon as he can,' he said. Gwen and Mary looked at each other. Bob Grant was the beat policeman.

Meanwhile, the broadcast upstairs was reaching new heights, as P.J. rocked and rolled with the best of them. Over by the leek bed, Robert was feeling distinctly out of it as he sat listening to Winston's radio, thinking of other things. If he hadn't been strapped in a wheelchair, though, he would have jumped sky-high when a pair of soft little hands gently covered his eyes from behind. He relished the moment before turning round to see Charlie and Hayley, standing there full of the joys of spring. He smiled full into Charlie's eyes. Hayley looked at them both, pulled a face and said goodbye gracefully. They didn't even notice.

'Hey!' said Robert. 'Hey, yourself!' said Charlie and they both smiled again. This was really the moment, this was when it started and they both knew and the smiles grew broader.

'How did you get on?' said Robert, when what he really wanted to say was that he loved her. But lads don't say things like that, sometimes not even when they've been married forty years. His smile said it for him and Charlie's smile said message received. 'It was great,' she said. 'What are you doing now?' And, without waiting for an answer, she seized the handles of the chair and quickly pushed him somewhere quiet where they could say things without being jeered at.

They talked as they went. It was as if they'd always known each other. Charlie looked at the back of his head and admired the way his thick black-brown hair curled and the pure white of his neck where he'd recently had a haircut. She very nearly bent down to give him a swift kiss but stopped herself in time, growing pink. They were there. She whirled the chair round to face her, then sat on the ground in front of him, crosslegged.

'What are they going to do with it, though, the song?' said Robert. She shrugged and pouted a bit.

'Don't know, to tell you the truth.' She wasn't quite sure she really trusted Mr Rettega. Hayley was taking him with a pinch of salt even though he had said they were going to cut a disc. Robert raised his eyebrows and she felt a sudden rush of tenderness.

'Cut a disc?' he said. 'That'll be the last we see of you, then.'

Charlie shook her head violently. 'No chance,' she said. Then he raised his eyebrow again and she suddenly felt shy. There was a little silence between them. When Charlie spoke, her voice came out very small. 'What do you do in the evenings?' He looked at her and she wished she could take the words back. Maybe she was being pushy. Oh, God, disaster! But his next remark made her feel better.

'Not much,' he said. 'Speedy sometimes takes us over to the Metro Centre. Bit of a performance on the train, though.' He looked at her. 'What about you?'

'Not much,' she said, keeping her eyes down. And her voice went even smaller. 'Er, do you want to go out sometime?' There was an awfully long silence and she winced. She'd ruined it, she knew she had. Then she ventured a look up and Robert was bright red too. But he was smiling broadly.

'I wouldn't mind,' he said and where her voice had been small, embarrassment was making his gruff. He cleared his throat. 'So long as you're not just taking pity on the poor cripple in the wheelchair.'

Her voice, as she replied, was the smallest yet. 'No, I'm not,' she said. 'I did at first, though.'

'Aye,' said Robert. 'I know. It shows. People think you're blind, deaf and dumb in these things.'

She nodded but he smiled again quickly. Everything was going to be all right. If she'd been closer, she would have given him a kiss. But there was plenty of time. No need to rush.

For the first time in many months, Robert started to think that there might be L.A.W. This was something his physio often talked about — life after wheelchair. Robert usually refused to even talk about it but Jenny, the physio, was always trying to make him face the thought that life would not just carry on the way it had before. She knew what Robert's idea of L.A.W. was. It was getting out of the chair and putting football boots on and scoring goals. His goals might have to be different, she said. The thought that those goals could include Charlie was very comforting. They chatted and Robert completely forgot his lookout responsibilities. Even when the police car went up the drive and stopped and PC Grant got out, it didn't register till Charlie spoke.

'What's Scuffer Grant want, d'you suppose?' she said. And, in the same instant, they both knew. 'Radio Rocket!' she said and her hand flew to her mouth.

'I'm supposed to be keeping me eye out!' said Robert and banged his knee in rage. She grabbed the chair and she started to wheel him up the path but he shook his head. 'Too late,' he said. 'Run round the side and give them a bellow in the side window!' She ran as fast as her twinkling feet could carry her and, even in his anxious state, Robert admired her flying figure. She got to the side of the Grove quicksticks, and attracted Speedy's attention by waving. Being Speedy, he just waved back. But Winston realised that something was up. He opened the window, heard what Charlie was saying, slammed the window back down and turned inside, his face white. P.J. looked at him.

'What?' said P.J. and Winston told him the police were outside. Within seconds, Radio Rocket was off the air, thoroughly ruining Jemma's afternoon. Jemma, Debbie's pain-in-the-bum little sister, had found out about Radio Rocket when she was pinching Debbie's Greenpeace T-shirt and she'd seen a poster giving the frequency. She'd gathered a gang of Brownies to listen and now they were blaming her because it had stopped too soon.

The radio room looked like a scene in a slapstick comedy film with Kelly and the lads running in all directions, hiding the gear. They finally got it all stowed away and made their way down the stairs with butter-wouldn't-melt expressions on their faces, although there was nearly a disaster anyway. P.J. was still wearing his headphone set, until Kelly noticed and ripped it off, nearly taking his ears with it.

But they needn't have bothered. PC Grant was just leaving. They stood and watched in a silent little knot until Geoff turned and saw them. 'What's up with you lot?' he said. 'Haway!' And haway they went, while Geoff shook his head yet again about the missing cash. He went back into his office and the rest went off to find something to quieten their nerves down.

Gwen was waiting in Geoff's office. 'What did the police-man have to say for himself?' she asked. Gwen wasn't that fond of policemen. Not that she'd ever had cause to doubt their efficiency or their goodwill, it was just that she couldn't see how anyone could do the job and remain normal. Imagine having to spy on your fellow creatures! Gwen couldn't. But it didn't stop her telling people off for eating meat and smoking. Like a lot of do-gooders, Gwen was a mass of contradictions. Not that Geoff had much to tell her anyway. Grant had listened, told him that one of the kids or one of the helpers was nicking the cash and the only way was to catch one of them doing it. Geoff knew all this already and it didn't make him feel any better to have this theory confirmed by the long arm of the law. So he just grunted at Gwen and she went out.

Things petered out at the Grove after that and most people went home early. Charlie pushed Robert all the way to his foster home, thus putting Speedy in an evil mood. Winston and Kelly went bowling. Duncan hung around to pay Carl back but Carl didn't come which meant that Duncan would owe him an extra day's interest. Carl was otherwise engaged. He got through the back and levered the hasp of the cellar door. Then he removed the video and screwed the hasp back on to give them a locked door mystery. Carl had an odd sense of humour. Spuggie went home to find Fraser. The secret was too big for her on her own now, especially since Beckett had hurt his foot. It was time to ask for help from big brother. And Geoff sat in his office and worried till it was time for him to lock up. Then he went home and worried. He didn't want it to be anyone he knew who was stealing the money. He also knew it had to be.

It had been a sort of turning point day, the kind of day people's lives change, the kind of day that Mary O'Malley's mother used to call a hinge day. You could look back, if you liked, in years to come and say to yourself, yes, that was the day it happened, that was the day I changed. Charlie and Robert fell in love, Geoff had to face a big problem. Alison made her mind up about something even if she wasn't quite sure what she'd decided. Speedy was going to run away to sea but that never came to anything, like a lot of what Speedy decided. Carl became a real thief. And Spuggie became a sister again when she got home and talked to Fraser.

'Where've you been?' he said. When she told him she'd been at the Grove, the rest of it came tumbling out. And Fraser was the way she'd always known he would be – kind and helpful and not a little excited. Especially when he realised she hadn't been stealing money off anyone. She showed him the telephone number written on her wrist and he smiled.

'Right!' said Fraser. 'Let's do it!' And Spuggie found that a trouble shared was a trouble halved and tucked her arm in his as they walked through the streets looking for a phone box.

Meanwhile, in a neat, expensive soulless, middle-class sort of house, the biggest change of all was happening. Michael Warner was watching his daughter pack a sleeping bag and a suitcase. He knew it was his fault that her mother had left but he wasn't man enough to tell anyone. He wasn't even man enough to tell himself. All he could do was work and eat and drink gin till he fell asleep and watch the daughter he used to love grow away from him.

For her part, Julie Warner had nothing but contempt for her father. He was a weak man. If he could have asked her for help or even for love, she might have been able to do something. But they didn't even talk to each other, except for good mornings that didn't mean anything and goodnights that smelled of hot, second-hand alcohol.

He watched her pack and she ignored him until he had to say something. 'And where are you going, miss, may I ask?' He couldn't even talk to her in his normal voice. He had to use that pompous, official voice, trying to keep his distance from the question to pretend it didn't matter and neither did the answer. She looked at him briefly and told him she was going to stay with a friend for a couple of days. She felt just a little pang as she saw the relief in his eyes.

'That's not a bad idea,' he said. 'I might have to go away myself for a couple of days . . . on business.' She nodded coolly, refused his offer of a lift and took the money he held

86

out. He stood awkwardly as she went to the door but all she did was turn and give him a cold cheek to kiss.

When she had gone, he poured himself a drink and sat down and thought of the fat, little chuckling baby she had been, always glad to see him. He looked at the telephone but decided not to ring anyone, not the girl she was going to stay with, not her mother, not anyone. Then he poured himself another drink.

Julie went across town on the bus and in a dream. When she got to Gill's house, she was so deep in thought, she wasn't sure where she was. She walked in and up the stairs as if she was floating, not sure whose legs she was using. Gill opened the door and his worried face made her laugh. He let her into the room and stood looking at her as if he was not sure why she was there. She dropped her stuff in the corner and held out her arms to him.

'I'm not sure this is a good idea, you know,' he said. But she stepped into the circle of his arms and closed his mouth with hers.

'Don't worry,' said the new Julie Warner, after a while. 'Don't worry. I'll make you sure.' And they kissed long and slow and deep until their heads swam and of all the things that had happened on this hinge day, this was the most important thing of all.

CHAPTER FIVE

Julie and Gill were living together, that was what it amounted to. It meant lots of good things and close times but it also meant missing out on some of the happiness they'd known at first. This might sound strange but the fact was that Julie found herself faced with a lot of unfamiliar hassles – doing the shopping and worrying about what to have for tea. Some of it was good fun, a bit like playing house, but some of it was a total bore, like going to the launderette, never having any money, not having much time to giggle with her friends. And Gill, never the most joyous person in the world even at the best of times, would sometimes lapse into long, deep silences and it was getting harder and harder to jolly him out of it. But there were still more good times than bad.

Julie was walking up the road to meet Gill at lunchtime and she smiled to herself as she fingered the plaited wristband she wore. They both wore them. They weren't married and they weren't engaged but they had made a commitment to each other and the plaited bands told the world. Well, they told that part of the world which understood such things – adults, teachers and parents not included. Julie's wristband had caused some raised eyebrows at break and Hayley had told her bluntly that she was a fool.

'You don't know what you're doing,' Hayley had said. 'Gillespie ain't exactly the steady kind. You going to get left some day. Make sure all you get left with is a bad memory not something that cries in the night!'

But Julie just smiled – she was sure of Gill. At that moment she saw him and ran and took his hand. He smiled at her. Payday meant that at least one of his constant worries had disappeared. Even though they didn't get much to live on, payday was still the best day of the week and they walked hand in hand by the river until Gill had to go back to work.

Donna and Nicola were back from Scarborough where they hadn't exactly spent the best holiday of their lives. There had been some minor mishaps, including a rainstorm which had flooded the caravan and soaked all Nicola's underwear. Donna, whose sense of humour leaned strongly towards the slapstick variety, had found this quite amusing. Her major problem on the holiday was Nicola's uncanny knack of always getting off with the best-looking lads. Twice Donna had been stuck with the wimp and once she'd had to spend half an hour fighting off an octopus under the bus shelter, while all she could hear from the other side was wild grunting sounds of passion. Nicola had had smug written all over her face when they went for the bus after. And she said they'd been doing nothing, which was a lot of horse feathers as far as Donna was concerned.

All in all, Donna was dead pleased to be home and even deader pleased to be going back to the Grove, where everybody knew their place, especially Nicola, whose place was clearly second to the Queen of Byker. On the way, she decided that Scarborough was going to be a closed book from now on. But she wasn't ready for the bombshell dropped by Nicola's pest of a sister. She stopped and looked at her, mouth open.

'Who's making a record?' she gasped. Debbie looked at her with the spite shining in her eyes, thought Donna. And who was Charlie, anyway? Marilyn Charlton from Denton Burn was who and she was making a record with Hayley Oduru. You couldn't turn your back for a second. She forgot about Scarborough not being a good topic of conversation and tried to turn the talk to what a good time they'd had. But Nicola, the cat, had already shot her mouth off about how miserable it had been, so that didn't work either. Feeling really fed up, Donna snapped at Brad and twitty

Gwen when they tried to get her interested in the Great North Run, and went into the Grove, thinking she might just as well have gone straight home. Right inside the door was the blonde bombshell herself, Miss Marilyn Charlton from Denton Burn, holding court with Nicola Dobson's mouth hanging open. Donna decided to walk right past and take stupid Nicola with her but Nicola shook her head and wouldn't come. Which left Donna feeling edgy.

'What's he like, though?' said Nicola and Charlie grinned and shrugged and simpered. Hayley deepened her voice and took the mickey which cheered Donna up. 'Who? Mr Rettega? Call me Steve, honey!' And they all laughed and Hayley went on to tell them about Mr Rettega and his gold chain and the video she was going to make with Charlie, stupid name! So Donna turned away, pretending she wasn't listening, and banged straight into Gwen who was still wittering on about the Fun Run and saving the planet and how many sponsors Donna could get.

Donna said she'd think about it, just to shut her up, and took the sponsorship form. Gwen nodded approvingly and then Donna went into the girls' loo and sprayed her hair with an aerosol can which didn't do the ozone layer any good at all. But it did Donna's hair and her morale a lot of good. She came out, looking outrageous, straight into a discussion of what the two budding songbirds were going to wear. She put a stop to that right off.

'Have you told them about them two lads we met at the seaside, Nicola?' she said. 'They were smashing, weren't they? The one that fancied me looked the dead spit of James Dean.' And she knew she'd clanged it when Hayley grinned and made a stupid joke about James Dean being dead long enough to be just about right for Donna. She sniffed and pointedly commented on Hayley's constant lack of boy-friends and again got it wrong. The smile on Hayley's face said, I know something you don't know, as clear as a bell.

Luckily, the lads came charging in just then and caused a

diversion. Brad looked up to see Robert leading a deputation. He started shaking his head as soon as he saw what they were carrying. It was a video cassette of 'Famous Cup Finals'. As they all knew, the video recorder was in quarantine because of all the fuss about Debbie Dobson watching the man with the rotting face and the finger knives. The lads protested strongly. Their most telling argument was that Geoff was on holiday and wouldn't find out. Brad weakened and eventually gave in, which was why Brad would never make a youth club leader. He still thought of himself as the same age as the kids he was looking after.

'All right,' he nodded. And the lads gave a cheer. He raised his voice to make himself heard. 'But I'm watching it with you, right?' He gave them the key and off shot Speedy and P.J. to get the machine from where Geoff had left it, locked in the cellar at the top of the steps.

Robert watched them go, his hands clutching the wheels of his chair. Brad saw the longing in his eyes and tapped his shoulder gently. Robert looked up, his eyes dark and full of memories. 'Soon, Robert,' said Brad and again he was quick enough to catch the swift sideways flicker of Robert's eyes to where Charlie was acting out her fantasy. Robert grimaced. 'Not soon enough for me,' he said. 'Not soon enough for me.'

'Brad nodded. He could see what the lad meant and tried to take his mind off things, jollying him along, telling him he should get involved in the Fun Run, then cursing himself as soon as the stupid words were out of his mouth. Robert just raised his eyebrows and looked down at his useless legs. Brad tried desperately to rescue the situation. The year before, there had been kids from a special school and they'd all had their wheelchairs done up like fighter planes, he told Robert hopefully. But Robert just grinned and said, a little bitterly, he was only in the chair for a short while and he didn't want to start thinking about himself and special schools. He was just someone who'd had a football accident

91

and he'd be out of it quick as a flash. Brad had nothing else to say and stood there feeling like a prune. But just then Charlie looked up. It must have been a radar. She saw Robert looking unhappy and she was there instantly.

'Don't you go upsetting my best friend,' she said to Brad and reached down to take hold of Robert's hand.

'Aye, right,' said Brad. 'Well, seein' as you're here and you're talking to a senior member of staff, you can stand to attention, Miss Prim!' Charlie nodded, saluted smartly and put her tongue out. Brad nodded back.

'Fine,' said Brad. 'Keep up the good work. And as a proper punishment for cheek, you are detailed to push this young man in the Fun Run.' Charlie looked at him.

'Give up,' she said, and Robert's heart sank, till he heard what came next. 'You don't think I'm going to let anyone else push him, do you?' she said. 'No fear! I'm far too jealous!' And she bent down and whispered something in Robert's ear which made him go red and, which is no business of anybody's except Robert's and Charlie's. Then she flirted her hips and went back to discussing her entry into the pop business.

Brad looked at Robert and grinned. 'Don't ask!' said Robert and grinned back. Brad looked around.

'Where have they got to with that recorder?' he wondered aloud.

Where they had got to was the top of the steps inside the cellar door. They had found two things. One was a broken lock. The other was no video recorder.

Down in the cellar itself, Beckett was dozing fitfully. His ankle was really painful, throbbing and difficult to move. He started, and shot awake at the sound of voices. He listened hard but couldn't make out what was being said. Then the cellar light went on and Beckett frantically forced himself behind the boxes at the back of the boilers. His lips peeled back over his teeth in a snarl of desperation. He looked up and, to his horror, saw Spuggie sliding through the window.

Forcing himself and his bad ankle across the floor, wincing at every step, he managed to get his hand over her mouth just in time.

'What . . .' she managed to get out before he muffled her words and motioned upwards with his hand. She saw the light on and her eyes widened. He took his hands from her mouth and they both crept over to the boxes.

At the top of the steps, Speedy and P.J. looked at each other. 'What was that?' said P.J.

'Nothing,' Speedy answered but his tone wasn't very convincing.

'I'm going to get Brad,' said P.J. and they walked off. But it wasn't long before they were both running.

Down in the cellar, Spuggie looked at Beckett, who jerked his head towards the stairs. She crept up slowly and was dismayed to find the broken lock. It had been unscrewed when Carl had stolen the video recorder but she didn't know that. All she knew was that her friendly Beckett was likely to be found if she didn't do something about the broken lock. Remembering that Fraser had a screwdriver in his toolbag on the bike, she slid back down the stairs and whispered her plan to Beckett. Then she went out of the window where Fraser was keeping a lookout. Her heart was beating like a drum. It couldn't go wrong now. Not now, when she'd finally got through to the man in Wales and made him understand that Beckett really needed help and that he had to come for him tonight.

Fraser was still outside the window, looking worried. 'What do you want me to do?' he exclaimed when she had finished telling him about the lock. He nodded as she told him and went around the front of the Grove to where his bike was. Just then PC Grant drove up. Fraser stopped stock still as he saw the policeman get out of his car and go towards the door. He stopped when he saw Fraser looking at him.

'Hello, young man,' he said. Fraser nodded weakly, then

waited till Grant had gone inside before taking the screw-driver out of his saddlebag and tiptoeing up the corridor to the cellar door. He started to work on the hasp as quickly as he could but cursed to himself as one of the screws dropped out of his fingers and rolled inside. He picked it up but sweat made his fingers slippery and he dropped it again. He stopped and took a deep breath to calm himself down. This was important – important for Beckett not to be found but even more important for Spuggie not to be connected to him and for the social worker to have no reason to come and visit the Campbells. For Fraser wasn't helping Spuggie to hide Beckett because he had romantic notions about the poor, hard-pressed fugitive. He was helping her in order to stop them both ending up in care. Otherwise, he would have shopped Beckett sooner than look at him. He finished his repair work, then slid down the corridor to the back of the building and out through the window.

As he went, P.J., Winston, Speedy and Kelly went tearing along the corridor, only to be stopped by Brad.

'Hey! Hey! Hey!' said Brad and they stopped and looked at him guiltily. P.J. and Speedy had been planning to tell him about the missing video recorder but it had soon become their very own exciting locked door mystery. Or unlocked door mystery, if you like. And so they'd decided to solve it themselves.

Brad adopted a very elaborate tone of voice. 'I thought . . . we were going to watch some FA Cup Final videos,' he said. 'Correct me if I'm wrong,' he added. They looked at each other.

'We're a bit busy now, Brad, man,' said Speedy. They all nodded.

'You have the attention span of a flea,' said Brad and would have left it at that. But a sudden thought struck him. He looked into their faces again, and what he saw made him ask the obvious question. 'So what have you done with the video recorder? His first thought was that butterfingers

Speedy had dropped it and his second thought was that Geoff would have his ears for wing mirrors for giving them the key in the first place.

P.J. came back down the corridor giving his best and most unconvincing P.J. smile. 'It wasn't there,' said P.J. and they all nodded again and made as if to go, Winston tossing a remark over his shoulder as he went. 'Geoff's probably took it home to watch *The Sound of Music* again.'

Brad took hold of Speedy's arm. 'OK,' he said. 'What have you done with it?' In the end, they managed to persuade him that the machine wasn't where it should be.

Just then, Grant the beat copper appeared and took in the scene. 'What's up?' he asked and they told him. 'Let's have a look,' he said and they led him to the door at the top of the cellar stairs.

Meanwhile, Fraser was round the back, looking for Spuggie. He didn't want to believe it but he knew she'd have gone back inside the cellar to keep Beckett company. He bent down to the window to hiss her name quietly, and was watched from the bushes by Carl, who was beginning to think that there was something very interesting hiding in the cellar.

Spuggie ignored Fraser and nestled close to Beckett. 'Don't worry. The door's locked again,' she said. 'And we've told your friend. He's bringing the car for you tonight. He'll flash his lights.' She thought for a minute. 'And you've got to bring the case. He said don't forget the case.'

Although she couldn't see it, Beckett's smile was bitter. He nodded, knowing that without the case and the money inside it, his 'friend' would not be driving through the night to rescue him. He had less friends than illusions, did Beckett.

Spuggie looked at him. She didn't want to ask the question but she had to know the answer. 'After you've gone away?' she said and stopped.

'What?' said Beckett.

'Do you think you'll ever come back here? To Newcastle?' There was a long silence and she had to swallow hard before she could say the next thing. 'I didn't think you would,' she said. 'Doesn't matter.' And she gave him a piece of paper with her name and address on it so that he could write and let her know how he got on. A feeling of tenderness like he had never known crept slowly over Beckett and he bent to kiss her on the top of the head, wishing he could take her with him and knowing at the same time that he was being stupid. A noise at the top of the stairs made him look up quickly.

The noise was Brad fingering the lock hasp. He looked at the lads, who looked blank. 'Someone's screwed it up again,' said Speedy.

Grant nodded. 'I'll get a prybar out of the car,' he said and went for it.

Fraser was getting fed up with trying to make Spuggie see sense so he wandered round the front of the building just in time to see PC Grant march purposefully back into the building carrying what looked like a crowbar. Word of what was happening had spread through the Grove and knots of people were beginning to gather. Fraser hurried back to the cellar window. This time he didn't bother hissing discreetly. He got his head as far inside as he could and bellowed for his sister.

'They're going to break the lock off,' he yelled. And they did. Beckett looked at Spuggie.'Go! Go!' she screamed. And he kissed her and struggled through the window with his case. The door burst open and they all crowded in for a look. Brad nodded. It was obvious that the video had gone. Grant sniffed the air. He jerked his head at Brad who turned and cleared everybody out. Brad turned back.

'What?' he said. Grant beckoned him down the steps and soon they were looking at what was left of Beckett's lair.

'You've had a lodger,' said Grant and Brad nodded. 'Tramp?' Grant nodded, then stiffened and picked up a little bit of paper. It was a piece of a bank wrapper used to wrap bundles of notes on which Beckett had written down the number Spuggie had first telephoned. 'Couldn't be,' said Grant half to himself, and turned with purpose to climb back up the stairs, followed closely by Brad.

Outside, Beckett was making slow and limping progress, watched by Fraser and Spuggie. She was almost in tears as she silently urged him on towards the wall. But Speedy, nosey as ever, came round the corner, saw Beckett and the case, and was off to raise the alarm before they could stop him. He was into the entrance hall with his news just as Grant and Brad came through the door. But he was so out of breath that at first he could only point. Then he managed to get it out.

'There's a feller hobbling off across the back with a big suitcase!' he said gleefully and rushed off to show them exactly where.

Bob Grant, who'd really only come down to the Grove to skive off and get a cup of Mary O'Malley's disgusting tea, was beginning to feel a distinct sense of excitement. The station had been buzzing for a couple of days. Two detective sergeants from South Wales had been in and a photofit of a shady character who was supposed to be on the run in Newcastle with a case full of iffy US dollars had formed part of the daily briefing only the day before.

Now, not a hundred yards away, was a shady-looking character with a heavy case getting over a wall. Grant radioed control as he ran towards the man who was limping heavily. He stumbled as he tried to climb the wall. The case flew out of his hand and burst open, spilling bundles of notes everywhere.

Beckett breathed deeply and turned to pick the case up. This was a bad move on his part, as Carl came up behind him, kicked him hard and accurately on his bad ankle and twisted his arm up his back as he sank to his knees in agony. Spuggie turned away. She couldn't watch. Nor could she watch as Brad reached Carl and Beckett and the two of them pinned him to the ground until the rest of the police arrived with the two sergeants from Wales.

They handcuffed Beckett, who kept his eyes turned firmly away from Spuggie, while the rest of the crowd goggled and chattered and chattered and goggled. Grant looked at Beckett.

'We thought you was miles away by now.' Beckett nodded and Grant looked at him keenly.

'I was delayed,' said Beckett.

'Don't suppose you feel like telling me who did the shopping, do you?' asked Grant and Beckett grinned at him. They put him in the car and it pulled away with Spuggie's eyes glued to Beckett and with his face just as firmly turned away. Fraser tugged her sleeve.

'Stop staring!' he whispered but she just pulled her arm away and wandered off, lost in her own silent thoughts, near to tears.

Brad was still high on the thrill of the chase. He turned to Grant. 'Who was he?' he said, surprised to find his voice sounding higher than normal and his hands trembling.

'High-class con man,' said Grant with satisfaction. 'And we think he was bringing dirty money for laundering.'

Brad shook his head. 'Doesn't make sense,' he said. 'Why was he hanging round here?'

Grant had the answer to that. 'We've been on the lookout at the stations and the airport. Probably waiting for a mate with a fast car and a passport to get him to the docks. Still —' And he paused. 'Doesn't solve the video mystery, does it?'

And even as he said it, he caught some byplay between Duncan and Carl. Duncan was staring at Carl accusingly and Carl was just as clearly glaring at Duncan, telling him to shut up. Carl saw that he was being observed and turned away quickly but not without a last glare at Duncan. Brad crossed over to Duncan who was still looking a little shaken and fearful.

'Come up to the office a minute, will you, Duncan?' he said and Duncan nodded, his eyes still fixed on Carl.

Fraser walked up to Spuggie and put his arm round her shoulders to lead her away. This time she let him do it. Her heart was too full for anything else. 'Careful,' he said under his breath and she nodded quickly to reassure him.

In the office, Alison and Brad and Gwen talked to Duncan slowly and carefully, trying not to frighten him and trying to find out what he knew about Carl and, more especially, the missing video recorder. They couldn't get any sense out of him at all, just stubborn repetitions that he didn't know anything. So they let him go but, just as he reached the door, Brad quietly said, 'Do you think it might be worth talking to Carl about our video recorder?' The effect was so shocking and startling that Alison shot Brad a quick look of utter reproach. The blood seemed to drain out of Duncan's face and his eyes shone like stars, glassy and bright. He breathed slowly and shallowly, obviously terrified. It was a little while before he could speak and then all he could do was stammer and plead with them not to say anything to Carl, to tell Carl that he hadn't said anything. It was very plain that Duncan thought Carl had stolen the thing and was scared that Carl would think he had grassed. They reassured him and let him go.

Then Brad rang Grant at the station and asked him what to do. Grant said he would float quietly by where Carl lived and have a quiet word with him, making sure he left Duncan out of it. But Carl was quicker than any of them.

He didn't have any faith in Duncan and he knew the sooner he got rid of the video, the better. He charged home through the back streets and, as he ran, he grinned to himself. He had thought of a very amusing way to get rid of the video.

Julie was surprised when Carl knocked at the door. She was even more surprised when he smiled at her. She'd never seen him smile before. She looked at him through the crack in the door.

'What do you want?' she said nervously. He nodded at the video he was carrying and held it out to her.

'I want to give Gillespie his machine back,' he said. She told him to put it down and he did so and went to his own room, watching through the crack in his own door as she picked it up and took it inside.

Gill was walking home wearily, going up the alley that led to the squat. He looked around as a police car overtook him and slowed down. It stopped alongside him and Grant looked out.

'Got a minute, son?' said the policeman and Gill waited. He had no great love for policemen. While he was growing up, there had been too many knocks in the middle of the night and too many hasty exits through the back door by his father for him to think a policeman could ever bring good news. He didn't say anything.

'Does a lad called Carl live anywhere round here?' asked Grant and Gill thought about it. Carl had a room on the same landing but the last thing Gill wanted was a busy on that landing seeing Julie and asking how old she was. He shook his head.

'Never heard of him, officer,' he said and started walking again. He could feel Grant watching him from the car so he just carried on walking past his own back door and on up to the main road.

Grant shook his head quietly to himself and looked at the blank windows with their tatty curtains. He couldn't see anybody watching him but he knew they were there. He also knew there wouldn't be many who would come to the door if he knocked. So he drove off. There's more than one way to skin a cat.

Gill went right round the front of the house and in through the front door. Julie was still kissing him hello when he saw the video recorder over her shoulder. When he heard where it had come from, he went and hammered on Carl's door. He had about as much success as the policeman would have had. Behind the door, Carl grinned to himself.

Gill had to wrap the recorder up in some newspaper, stick it in a big carrier bag and smuggle it out. Luckily, there was a builder's skip at the end of the street. The houses were being bought cheap and renovated by people with more taste than money. There was always a builder's skip at the end of the street. Gill knew the video machine wouldn't be there long.

Then he went back in and had a row with Julie about it. All in all, it wasn't a good day for the Byker Grove clientele. Unless you count Carl, who had had several chuckles.

At the police station, Beckett drew long and hard on the cigarette the CID men had given him. He had a decision to make and it wasn't going to be easy. The two men from Wales had been working on him, trying to get him to confess, playing good guy and bad guy, alternately. Beckett had heard it all before He was fairly certain he was going to jail. The prospect didn't bother him. But he wanted to do something for Spuggie's first.

'If I cough to this?' he said and stopped. The two CID men looked at each other. One of them told the tape-recorder there was going to be a break for refreshment, then switched it off. Beckett told them he would hold his hands up to the offences he was accused of, if they would make sure Kirstie Campbell and her family got some help from the social services. They wrote his confession down and he signed it. Then they took him to Lancaster Prison. They left a note about Spuggie for PC Grant.

And Spuggie lay awake, face down on her wet pillow, wishing she could still be with Beckett.

CHAPTER SIX

Gill and Julie rowed all night, each one accusing the other of being selfish. And they let the sun set on their anger and it was so late when they finally went to sleep still bickering that they overslept and when they did wake up, things went from worse to worse. While Gill rampaged round, trying to find a clean T-shirt, Julie opened the curtains and looked out over the less than picturesque neighbourhood. He came back in and looked at her. She looked back and she knew the look on her face was the one that had never failed to get right up her parents' noses – blank and insolent.

'You were stupid,' said Gill. 'If that copper had found that video in here, we'd have had it. I was just quick enough to get it out. Only just.' Julie paused for a moment before replying and her voice was as sarcastic as she could make it.

'My hero,' she said bitterly and turned away. He controlled his temper with an effort.

'Isn't it time you got ready for school?'

She turned again and spoke slowly. She didn't know why she was doing it; she was taking delight in picking her words, trying to hurt him, like picking a scab until it bled. 'You sound like my mother,' said Julie. And she considered him. 'You've got the same tight little lips.' His lips did tighten at this, she saw – with satisfaction. I'm not going to school today, she went on and he carried on dressing in silence. Then he looked up. She saw the hurt in his eyes and was immediately sorry for what she'd done.

'Don't cut me to pieces,' he said softly. 'Just because you're not happy.' And she took him into the warmth of her arms and they held each other in silence.

'You should shout back,' she said and leaned back to smile full into his face. He nodded. He would. But . . .

'But what?' she said and he shook his head until she held it with both her hands and made him tell her.

'If I shout at you,' he said, and he could hardly get the words out. 'If I shout at you, I'm afraid you might go away from me for good.' She kissed him again and held him again and promised not to go away. The mood was broken almost at once by the sound of a car horn – it was Billy Mac who'd been sent to get Gill. He rushed out.

Go to school,' he said as he left. 'Won't you?' She smiled and said she'd think about it and the last tender gesture of the morning was Gill waving his fist in mock anger as he got into Billy Mac's old banger. She watched out of the window until she noticed Carl watching her. She flushed and drew her dressing gown together. He applauded in mime and blew her a kiss. Drawing the curtains quickly, she started to get dressed. Whatever she wore, when Carl was about, it didn't seem like enough. She really didn't want to go to school, though. She'd just get dressed and go round the shops, maybe call in on Gill at work and have a sandwich with him at lunchtime. The thought brightened her up and she hurried to get ready.

When she was dressed, she looked round the room and winced a little at the general mess. One thing neither she nor Gill were much good at was tidying up. She poked a few things around and then went out. She could tidy up some other time. She could spend the rest of her life tidying up if she wanted to. Today she was going to bunk off school. And when she went out and Carl wolf-whistled, she gave him the arm and the whistle died halfway through. It was replaced by a grin, though, at her back. More to the princess than meets the eye, Carl thought to himself and he wondered just how long she'd stay with Gillespie the drip. Not long, was Carl's guess. Not long.

The pressure on Winston to get his dad's portable car telephone had by now reached such a pitch that he was beginning not to want to go to the Grove ever again. P.J., Robert, Speedy, they were all giving him earache all the

103

time. And even Kelly, who he could normally trust to be on his side, had started with the little snide remarks. And then she'd backed him right into a corner. Which was how they found themselves at dinnertime with no dinner inside them, standing just inside the open-air market by the river watching a spieler pulling a crowd round him. Kelly nudged Winston.

'I thought we were coming to ask your dad to borrow his telephone.' Winston nodded and indicated the shouting man. Kelly was amused and amazed. 'Is that your dad?' she asked and watched, fascinated.

'He says he is,' Winston grunted. 'I haven't been able to prove he's not, yet!'

Kelly giggled and held on to his arm. She really liked Winston no matter what anybody said. They moved closer and the spieler clocked them out of the corner of his eye. Before Kelly knew what was going on, he was using them in his spiel, pretending he didn't know them, had never met them before, and they were genuine customers.

His patter was electric, quickfire and funny. The customers were rocking and laughing at his sallies and he was selling his goods quicker than Kelly had ever seen anyone do anything, except perhaps once when she had gone with her father to a livestock auction. Winston's father's attack was very like the auctioneer selling cows and sheep, like a machine gun going off. When it was all finished, he called Winston over and Kelly saw just how much they liked each other, even though they pretended they didn't. Winston got a five-pound note for helping out and Kelly was introduced as a friend. Winston's dad nodded and smiled. Kelly poked Winston's ribs. 'Ask him,' she whispered but Winston shook his head.

'Ask me what?' said Winston's dad, as sharp in his hearing as he was in everything else.

'Nothing!' insisted Winston but Kelly poked him again. 'He wants to know,' she said, 'if we can borrow your mobile telephone.' The telephone was Winston's father's pride and joy and it showed on his face.

'What do you want it for?' he demanded and Winston had to improvise in a hurry.

'We're doing a project at the Grove,' he said. 'And – er – Geoff wants to show everyone a mobile telephone.' There was a little silence while they all looked at each other. He went on lamely. 'So we'll know what one looks like.' His father nodded.

'You,' he said, 'are the worst liar I have ever met in my entire life. How do you expect to make a living on a stall if you can't even tell proper lies? I'm convinced you're not my son. You can't be!'

Then Kelly took a hand and told him that they wanted to borrow the phone to run a phone-in on a pirate radio station and she was going to be the agony aunt. There was more silence and Winston waited for the storm to break all over the two of them. But Winston's dad roared with laughter, ruffled Kelly's hair and asked Winston why he couldn't make up fibs like that. Then he lent them the telephone and told them if they so much as scratched it, they were dead. He went off for more gear, still laughing.

'I like your dad,' said Kelly and they went off to catch the bus.

Geoff was being faced with another to add to his mounting store of problems. He saw himself as a sort of unofficial father, teacher, helper, scoutmaster, call it what you like, to the kids who went to the Grove. Part of his value to them was the fact that they could talk to him about any problem, and he never took sides. He might point out a few alternatives, he might give you a rollicking, he might even, in certain circumstances, lend you a pound. But earache was not on the menu unless deserved. You could always rely on Gwen or Mary O'Malley for that, anyway.

Now, Geoff put the telephone down with a sigh and ran

his fingers along his moustache. Gwen, who was busy sorting out the arrangements for the Junior North Run, looked at him anxiously.

'What?' she said. 'Bad news?' He nodded at the phone.

'Bob Grant,' he said. And stopped and looked at her. She asked what about Bob Grant, who was of course PC Grant and the man who had got the message from Beckett about Spuggie and Fraser and his worries about the Campbell household. Geoff told Gwen what had been reported and she looked at him and shook her head.

'I'm sorry,' she said. 'I don't see what your problem is. Tell Mrs Meade and she can go round and have a looksee.'

Mrs Meade was the social worker and, obviously, there was a good deal of unofficial contact between all the staff at the Grove and her department. She was a nice woman with a stern expression that belied her genuine fondness for children. Geoff shook his head.

'I'll need to find out a bit more about it. I've got a feeling Campbell's done a runner. If his missus is all right, there won't be a problem but —'. He shook his head again and tilted an imaginary bottle to his lips. 'Last time he disappeared, she fell straight into a bottle a day of sweet white wine.'

Gwen looked disapproving. People who drank were quite beyond the pale in her book, and this put the question beyond doubt. Geoff had to tell the social worker and if the children ended up in care, it would probably be the best thing all round.

Spuggie and Fraser had been discussing the same problem. Betty Campbell was getting vaguer and vaguer every day. They knew they would have to get the doctor in soon. The trick would be to get the doctor on his own, though, without having him bring the social worker in. They both had a horror of being taken into care. They didn't want to leave their home; most of all they didn't want to leave their mother. Most of the time she was fine, Fraser thought to himself bitterly, but she'd been getting hold of wine. At first, it had been just a couple of drinks to help her to get to sleep but now he was finding bottles everywhere. And she kept forgetting things. If the doctor could just give her something to help her sleep, then she wouldn't need the booze and she'd soon be back on her feet. They could look after her, there was no need to involve anyone else.

Out at the leek bed, Alan Dobson, proud father of Nicola, Debbie and Jemma, would have looked on the practice of putting children in care with a great deal of interest at that particular moment. Unluckily for him, the youngest, Jemma, had just grown big enough and important enough in her own eyes to want to join Byker Grove, where the other two were happily in place. Happily, that is, as long as they were out of each other's sight. Like a lot of sisters, they weren't really happy in each other's company. Or, to put it another way, they hated the sight of each other. The thought of having all three of them complaining about the same thing at the same time and in the same place would have brought a lesser man to his knees. But Alan Dobson was made of good stuff. His two hobbies were growing leeks and playing the drums and they'd fitted him pretty well for most of life's little troubles. Except the one that was nearing flashpoint right at this very minute.

Middle sister, Debbie, had come out of the Grove with blood in her eye and made a beeline for Jemma who was already high in the stakes for a major pain-in-the-bum award. Jemma saw her coming and started to talk very fast about the need for someone keen to look after the leeks. After a short pause, she thought out loud that maybe what was needed was someone called Jemma, about her age and about her size. Debbie looked her straight in the chest. 'What are you doing in my T-shirt?' she said menacingly. Jemma looked down as if surprised to find what she was wearing.

'The tumble-dryer's broke,' she said and started to talk about leeks again but Debbie wasn't going to be put off by a tumble-dryer. She called her father into the argument but Alan was more interested in the state of the leeks. He looked at them closely while the T-shirt argument raged. Eventually he shut his two daughters up by pointing out that he owned all the T-shirts, having paid for them with his hard-earned cash, and if the row didn't stop at once all T-shirts would be grounded and they'd have to wear school blouses for a fortnight. The two girls stomped off to hate each other from a distance, while he kneeled down to look at the leeks, one of which was split.

Winston and Kelly went past, Winston going faster when he saw Alan Dobson at the leek bed. But Alan looked up just in time to see him and called him over. Winston went slowly and unwillingly, with Kelly on his arm. She was keen to see if Winston's leek food had done any good. She looked at Winston fondly. He had such good ideas.

'Winston,' said Alan Dobson. 'Have you seen anyone hanging round these leeks?' Winston shook his head hastily. He hadn't seen anyone, he hadn't been near them himself and he was very sorry, he had to go now. Beside him, he could feel Kelly opening her mouth to tell Alan about the wonderful plant food she had seen Winston putting on the leek bed so he tugged her arm and they disappeared at a fast trot with Kelly still trying to get her mouth open. Alan Dobson looked at them and shook his head. Kids!

Jemma came smiling back. 'That lad was carrying a mobile telephone,' he remembered. Then Debbie arrived as well, still seething. 'What do they want a mobile phone for, Debs?' he asked. She tossed her head. She didn't know which was worse, being called Debs or having to watch her poisonous little wart of a sister wearing her new Elefriend T-shirt. 'Don't know,' she said ungraciously.

Jemma smiled. 'I do,' she said. They looked at her, waiting for the answer, but she just smiled annoyingly. 'It's a secret,' she said just as annoyingly and waltzed off.

In the meantime, Donna's natural high spirits were

coming out again. It would take more than a wet week in Scarborough to dampen Donna and she was now heavily engaged in taking the mickey out of Nicola's sincere regard for the environment, which had started off as veggie and quickly gone on to saving the whale and worrying about holes in the ozone layer.

Donna was scathing. 'I don't want to save a whale,' she said. 'I wouldn't know where to put it, if I did, would I?'

Nicola rolled her eyes in exasperation. 'It's all right laughing at everything, Donna,' she said. 'But this is serious. The whole planet is in danger if we don't do something about it.'

Donna pulled a face. 'Don't look at me,' she said. 'I haven't touched the planet.'

Nicola still couldn't see that Donna was just mocking her, and carried on hotly. 'It's not just you,' she said. 'It's everybody! We've all got to stop driving about and ruining the ozone layer with carbon stuff.'

There was a little pause and Donna's eyes gleamed. 'Anyway,' she said, using what was, to her, the final argument, 'lads don't like vegetarians. Where's he going to take you? I still haven't got over you asking that waiter in Scarborough if there was any animal stock in tomato soup.'

Nicola pursed her lips. 'I just don't want to compromise my principles,' she declared primly.

Donna smiled again, just a shade maliciously. 'You compromised them under the bus shelter,' she said. 'I heard you!'

Nicola was cross and delighted at the same time. She remembered what had happened under the bus shelter. (She also remembered what had nearly happened, but that's nobody's business except Nicola's.)

'I did not!' she exclaimed. 'I did not!'

'You were halfway down that Gary's throat,' teased Donna. 'I could hear you! You sounded like a vacuum cleaner!'

Nicola grinned. 'I was not,' she said. 'And what difference would it have made, anyway?' She tossed her hair and grinned again, remembering.

Donna played her trump card. 'He'd been eating a beefburger,' she said. Nicola knew what was coming next. 'There would have been some fat round his mouth. Bound to be.' And she added the final point with relish. 'Animal fat!'

Nicola screamed and hooted and they punched each other, rolling about laughing.

The laughter stopped as Charlie arrived with a face like tripe. Her usual sunny grin was missing and Donna leapt on her like a hungry shark, her voice impossibly sweet.

'Hey up!' she said. 'What's wrong with Kylie today. How's the recording contract going, Charlie?' As always, Charlie's face reflected what was going on inside.

Donna smiled in apparent sympathy. 'I told you it wouldn't work, didn't I? I told you my dad said that Steve Rettega was all mouth and trousers, didn't I?' He hadn't said anything of the sort as a matter of fact but Donna never let the truth get in the way of a smart remark. Charlie's face didn't get any brighter. It wasn't exactly what had happened that was bothering her, it was what was going to happen.

To find that out, you need to know what kind of guy Steve Rettega really was. Bright and not too honest and very keen on the main chance would sum him up pretty correctly. He had been very taken with the idea of the two kid singers at first. But as he watched what they could do, he realised pretty quickly that the real moneyspinner wasn't the one black, one blonde duo he'd had in mind. The real star was Charlie. He had to get rid of Hayley and he had to do it without Hayley realising it or she might pull up paving stones. Hayley had a quick temper and Hayley was shrewd.

But Rettega was shrewder and in his stable of singers and bands he had a blue beat combo, dreadlocks and slim hips, led by a streetwise black man a little bit older than Hayley.

And Steve had a word with Vas Takedeli who waited outside one evening, switched on his big smile and made Hayley an offer she couldn't refuse. So Hayley had stopped Charlie outside school and told her the bad news, which had made Charlie's chin hit the floor. And instead of going home, she had gone straight to the Grove, looking for sympathy. If she had gone home, of course, she would have found a message from Steve telling her not to worry. But life's not like that. And Donna was sharpening her little claws for the attack when a sudden thought struck her. As Charlie went on moaning about Hayley dropping out and ruining everything, Donna swallowed and smiled sweetly, backtracking as fast as she could.

'Steve Rettega's not that bad, though, is he?' she said.

Nicola looked at her open-mouthed. She'd seen Donna change her mind before, of course, but the speed of this U-turn was truly terrifying.

Donna cut Nicola off before she could say anything and set about persuading Charlie that if stupid Hayley wasn't available for record-making the Grove's answer to Sinead O'Connor would gladly step in and help her out. The discussion went on for quite some time.

Meanwhile, in the other corner Spuggie wilted in and got the chessboard out. She was laying the pieces on it when Geoff came past.

'I didn't know you could play chess,' he said with one of his best smiles. Spuggie looked up and sniffed.

'There's lots people don't know about me,' she retorted. She put a knight down and nodded at it with satisfaction. Geoff sat down across the table and looked at her from under his eyebrows until she had to look up and give him a little grin. He grinned back.

'Fancy a game?' he said.

'I didn't know you played chess,' she said, echoing him impishly and he played the ball right back to her.

'Oh, aye,' he said. 'There's lots people don't know about

111

me.' And they set to and played a game and he found himself marvelling, as Beckett had in the allotment shed and in the dark, dusty cellar. He found himself marvelling at her speed of thought and the quick wit of her game. Through the game, he tried his hardest. He wasn't a player, really, and she soon backed him into a corner, took his queen and checkmated him with a cry of triumph. He looked at her and shook his head. 'You sucked me in, didn't you?' he said and she laughed at him in sheer delight.

'Not me,' she said. 'Not me! It was the knight!' And her blue eyes shone as she looked at the little horse and she remembered what Beckett had said. 'He hopskipped his way through and made way for the bishop like a broadsword! Flash!' she said. 'And the queen was gone! And the king!' She stopped. The king was gone all right and he'd left the queen behind. He was never coming back and her eyes grew darker and her mouth set in a tight line. She didn't want to cry again. She'd done enough crying to last her forever.

Geoff patted her hand gently. 'I know, pet,' he said. 'I know!' And she flashed back at him that he knew nothing. Nobody knew anything. And she looked down at the board and suddenly sent the pieces flying as she stood up. Geoff pulled her down gently. 'Mr Beckett told the police how you helped him,' he said softly but she just pulled herself away.

'He wouldn't!' she said. 'He didn't!' and stood, looking at Geoff with big eyes. She realised she'd given herself away. Geoff spoke gently.

'It's all right, pet,' he said. 'I'm not telling anyone. Is everything all right at home?' She looked at him and he hung on, waiting, hoping to get the chance to do something for the two Campbell kids. He knew she was just about to let the floodgates open when in came Fraser who saw what was happening.

'Come on, Spuggie,' said Fraser. 'You've not forgotten, have you, we're going to the pictures tonight. And then me mam's taking us for a Macdonald's.' And he looked Geoff

112

straight in the eye, daring him to challenge the lie. Then Fraser went out with Spuggie and Geoff knew he'd lost a real chance to do something.

In his office, he picked the telephone up and rang Mrs Meade, the social worker. She'd been to see Fraser and Spuggie before and she said as much, but Geoff managed to persuade her to come and have a chat as he thought the circumstances had changed. He put the phone down and looked at Gwen. He felt like Judas Iscariot and even though she assured him that someone had to do it, it didn't make him feel any better.

Then the phone went again and it was Rettega, the smooth operator, making sure that it was all right for Gwen to go down to the studio with Charlie. He said it was and put the phone down to find Gwen shaking her head. He stared at her. 'What?' he said. She told him she had no intention of going down to the studios any more, the music gave her a headache. And she stormed out, leaving Geoff to shake his head. He wasn't too worried, though. Hayley would be with Charlie after all and Hayley was sixteen and Hayley had her head screwed on. He didn't know that Hayley wasn't part of Rettega's plans any more or he might have made sure that there was someone to go with Charlie. And a lot of grief would have been spared. But that's hindsight and hindsight is the most exact science in the world.

Donna was still plugging hard to take Hayley's place but Charlie wasn't proving quite as keen as Donna would have liked. Finally and firmly, she told Donna that she wasn't going to ask Rettega if Donna could take Hayley's place which sent Donna banging out through the door like a whirlwind. Nicola pulled a face and, after a moment, so did Charlie.

'I wouldn't mind,' said Nicola, but she's got a voice like a crow!'

And through the giggles came Donna's voice from the other side of the door. 'That's the last time I talk to you,

113

Dobson, that's for sure,' she said and Charlie rolled around and so did Nicola as they leaned on each other, laughing. Geoff came over and looked at the heaving heap.

'What's up?' he said but they were too far gone to say anything so he just shook his head and passed over the message about the photograph session at the studio with Rettega. This stopped the laughter and Charlie's face grew glum again. She looked at Nicola but Nicola shook her head, knowing what she was going to ask.

'I can't,' said Nicola. 'She's my best mate and if I went with you down to the studio, it'd really be like betraying her. I can't.'

Charlie nodded and went outside, her face solemn enough for Robert to be concerned. He was sitting in his wheelchair, listening to Radio Rocket, grinning to himself as he heard P.J. trail the agony aunt that they were going to broadcast, giving the telephone number of Winston's dad's phone, but Charlie's face drove all that out of his mind.

'What's up with you?' he said. 'You look terrible.' And she told him all her woes, how she couldn't go to the studio and how Hayley had dropped out and everything was falling to pieces. He thought about it. Robert was a deep thinker. He'd had lots of time to practise, after all, flat on his back after the football injury that had landed him in the wheelchair in the first place. One thing didn't make sense to Robert.

'If Hayley's dropped out and Rettega knows?' he said and stopped.

Charlie looked at him. 'What?' she said.

That meant, as far as Robert could see, that Rettega still wanted Charlie to go on with it or why would he want her down the studios to take photographs? Charlie thought about this and her face cleared slowly and then clouded just as quickly. She still didn't have anyone to go to the studio with. Her mum wouldn't let her go without a chaperone. And her mum was working late anyway.

'I'll go with you,' offered Robert and then took it back just

114

as quickly. 'Not that I'd be any good in a crisis.' He picked at the wheel rims. She shook her head.

'It's on the third floor,' she said. 'We couldn't get you up the stairs.'

'No,' he agreed and thought about it. He really did want to go. 'I could stop outside and if you were longer than we agreed, I could ring someone up.'

She could see how much he wanted to go and she wanted him to be there too. Nothing was going to happen anyway. It was as simple as that. They agreed and, being kids and fully in control of their own destinies, they didn't bother to tell anyone what they were going to do.

So, that evening, Charlie dressed to kill and Robert grinning to please, they set off, hand in wheelchair for the Riverfront Recording Studios, ready to fall in love or make their fortunes or just to have a good time. And she kissed him outside the door for the first time and they checked their watches, laughing at themselves for doing it, and in she went.

And Robert settled down to worry outside.

And, at the Grove, in the radio room, Radio Rocket went on the air and it was the funniest evening any of them had ever had. Kelly was in the agony aunt chair, ready and willing to discuss any little intimate problems the younger inhabitants of Newcastle upon Tyne might need advice on. She was worried about drying up so Speedy brought her a glass of water and P.J. rolled his eyes and sharpened his best DJ manner and set the ball rolling.

About a mile away, with a handful of ten-pence pieces and a wicked sense of humour, Nicola and Donna were all set to play the joke of a lifetime on Kelly, who was sitting wide-eyed and bushy-tailed in Byker Grove and never expecting for a minute to get a call from a couple of novice nuns who were about to give up their faith. Which was what Donna and Nicola had decided to be. Just for the

115

purposes of the telephone call, you understand. Nothing heavy.

At the recording studios, Charlie was in seventh heaven, on cloud nine and swinging on a star, if you'll pardon the clichés. Mrs Rettega was there, taking the photographs, and Steve had told her just why they were needed. He was going to make her a star. She would be on *Top of the Pops*, she would be famous. It's hard to be too condemning of Charlie. She was only fifteen, the lights were flashing, the music was playing and she was singing her heart out. Time passes quickly when you're having fun, as they say. Time passed quickly for Charlie. Time had lead boots on for Robert, sitting outside and chewing his fingernails. They'd agreed, he and Charlie, that she wouldn't be any more than an hour and if she was going to have to be longer than that, she'd come down and tell him that everything was all right.

Robert sat and looked at the iron door and the blank windows. The hour passed and then another twenty minutes and then another fifteen minutes dragged their way past, every second beating like a drum, every beat of the drum telling Robert that something was seriously wrong and that Charlie, without a chaperone, was in serious bother with the rat-smooth Steve Rettega. He set his wheelchair rolling and went round the corner to look for help. But there was no help anywhere to be had. And the first telephone box he came to was smashed and the second had a little step to it. He couldn't get close enough in the chair. He tried backing in, he tried coming at it sideways on. Nothing. And all the time, he could see Charlie's face, mouth open wide in terror, screaming a silent scream that only he could hear. He tried to make himself taller in the chair, bracing his arms, ignoring the pain in his back and his neck. Nearly. He braced himself again. Not quite.

And upstairs, Charlie looked at Rettega.

'One more time!' said Steve. He was nearly as excited as

116

Charlie and his wife grinned to see him. He hardly looked any older than Charlie when he got carried away like this. And she swung into it once more.

On the pavement outside, Robert gathered himself for one final effort. But he hadn't locked his wheel brake and, as he grasped the telephone at the final attempt, the wheelchair shot away from under him, smashing his head against the pavement, jarring his neck unmercifully and sending him unconscious into the gutter.

Steve Rettega looked at his watch and as he did so, a cold hand seemed to clench itself round Charlie's heart.

'What time is it?' she managed to gasp before looking at the clock herself and getting the answer. Without another word, she barged past Steve and Mrs Rettega and was down the stairs like a rocket. They followed her, looking at each other, shrugging.

She stumbled and fell the last few steps and couldn't open the door, banging at it in her fright and frustration. Rettega caught up with her and tried to turn her round but she just beat at him with her fists until he gave in and opened the door, following her as she ran out and down the street and round the corner. He followed her and found her on her knees, sobbing by Robert's silent figure. He took one look at the pale face and the deep shadows under the eyes and reached over Charlie to the telephone, dialling for the ambulance. Then he bent down to try to pick Robert up, only to be beaten away again by her small hard fists.

'Leave him alone,' she said. 'Don't touch him. It's his spine!' He nodded and stood back, knowing the ambulance would soon be there.

But the ambulance took forty-five minutes because the radio link was constantly interrupted and blanked out by the merry voices of P.J. and Kelly and Donna and Nicola.

When the ambulance finally made it, the two paramedics took one look at Robert. One of them met Rettega's eyes

117

and shook his head slightly and nodded at Steve to take Charlie away. She fought and didn't want to go.

'Where have you been?' she screamed at them. 'Where have you been?'

But nobody answered and they took Robert away.

CHAPTER SEVEN

Robert didn't die. Although for a long time, the doctors were shaking their heads. It was touch and go and if it hadn't been for the skill and dedication of the ambulancemen, there would have been tears and flowers and a funeral in the corner of the North-East which contains Byker Grove and all the people that go there. Geoff was in a quiet, blind rage for days. He didn't mind kids playing up, he didn't mind breaking windows; anything like that sprang out of high spirits, young enthusiasms, things that should be encouraged. But Radio Rocket had been inspired and run by the best brains at the Grove and that was all the harder to forgive and forget.

P.J. and Speedy and Winston and Robert himself should have known that what they were doing was wrong and ought to have realised that pirate radio stations aren't just banned out of official bloody-mindedness but because the airwaves they interfere with are used by the caring services. The first Geoff had known that nearly fatal evening had been Charlie sweeping up the stairs, blind with tears. Geoff and Alison had followed and found her kicking the radio equipment to pieces, spitting and swearing and attacking the operators.

Then, when he'd managed to calm her down, Rettega had arrived and they'd got the full story. Any kind of disciplinary action wasn't necessary. Those involved with Radio Rocket knew what they'd done and they knew they'd nearly killed Robert and the air at the Grove was quiet and gloomy.

It wasn't helped by the talk Geoff had had with Mrs Meade, the social worker. He confided his suspicions to her about Spuggie and Fraser's father having done a runner and Mrs Campbell not being altogether with us. Mrs Meade had promised to go and see what could be done and so she did and went back to report to Geoff. She went to the flat and couldn't get in, although there was somebody moving about

119

inside. She went next door to see what information there was available. Not much, was the short answer from the bright-eyed, nosey neighbour but she found out that Mr Campbell hadn't been seen for quite some time.

Good riddance to bad rubbish!' snorted Mrs Next-Door but such opinions can't always be relied on, as Mrs Meade knew very well. Bad relations between next-door neighbours are often only the result of loud noises late at night. And that's often just due to people being bored with no work to go to in the day and staying up late watching the telly. But she told Geoff she'd keep an eye on it and he was to tell her if things changed. She was almost sure she'd seen the two kids herself as she came out of the block of flats.

She had, but Fraser and Spuggie – always wary of social workers –had seen her too, then scarpered. Meanwhile, their mother's illness hadn't been getting any better and they eventually had to face up to the fact that they had to get the doctor. Fraser didn't want to go to the health centre again, having had a run-in with the snotty receptionist once before, so he got out the phonecard they'd used to try to get help for Beckett from his friend in Wales. Spuggie looked at the card as Fraser told her what he was going to do.

'Don't use it all,' she muttered. Fraser knew why she wanted to keep some of the phonecard. She was going to try to find out where Beckett was and get in touch with him. He was angry.

'He's not coming back, Spuggie,' he said. 'He's not coming back. You might just as well forget him.' But she just looked at him with dead eyes.

'Don't use it all,' she said again stubbornly and Fraser breathed out hard. He knew he was never going to get her to see sense and he resolved to throw the card away as soon as he'd managed to get hold of the doctor. He came back from the phone box.

'He's going to come this afternoon,' he said. 'I've told them she's very ill.' She was. She wouldn't get out of bed and occasionally she moaned in pain. She wouldn't eat anything, and only drank the odd cup of tea. They'd stopped getting any cheap white wine, mainly because they didn't have any money for anything other than food but also because Mr Rao at the little off-license had started asking awkward questions too. Spuggie looked at Fraser.

'She won't answer the door,' she said and he nodded. 'You'll have to stop off school,' he said. 'It's your turn. I'll do you a note.' Fraser was an expert at forging notes and often made a couple of bob at it for friends who needed a day off and didn't need the truant officer.

So Spuggie was left at home through a long morning. She did her best to tidy the flat but it was still not in the best of conditions when the doctor came. Dr Kerr looked around and noted the shabbiness. The furniture had seen its best days long since, the curtains had been washed to rags and the next washing would probably put holes in them. It was only the dirt that held them together. The little girl though – he looked at his notes to check her name, Kirstie – the little girl was putting a good face on things. Her hair was clean, her clothes clean too, and she was obviously planning to keep herself that way.

In the bedroom, it was a different story. Spuggie had managed to get her mother into a clean nightie and had plumped the pillows up when she heard the knock at the door. But Mrs Campbell's condition made the doctor frame a silent whistle which he hid quickly as he saw the little girl's sharp eyes flicker towards him. He did pulse and temperature checks but they just confirmed what he already knew. He picked up the empty tranquilliser bottle to check the date, pondered a minute and then looked at the daughter. She was looking at him fearfully but quickly managed to change her expression to one of blankness.

'I should get hold of your father,' he said and her reply was quick and pat.

'He's at work,' Spuggie said. 'Eckton's,' she added before he could ask.

He nodded and asked what time the man would be home, knowing the answer already. But the little girl kept up the pretence that her father would be home later that day even though his receptionist knew all the local gossip and had told him there was little chance of the father being seen again for a very long time. He looked at the patient once more and then went to wash his hands. She was very underweight and barely hanging on to what life there was left in her frail frame. He doubted if she'd eaten anything for some time and he'd already decided to admit her to whichever hospital had a bed.

'Your mother's going to have to go into hospital for a bit,' he told the little girl. She just took the information as if she'd known what was coming and she absorbed the next piece of information in the same way, looking at him carefully but giving nothing away.

'I'll – er – I'll get Mrs Meade to come and have a word with you,' he went on. Spuggie nodded. She knew who Mrs Meade was. The doctor looked at her again, trying to gauge what else needed to be said. In the end, he just went to the door. He was a busy man and had lots more calls to make before afternoon surgery. As he left, the postman arrived with a parcel which Spuggie took off him. She closed the door, her mind racing. And, long before she'd unwrapped the parcel, she knew what she was going to do.

She went into the bedroom to see her mother and tell her the ambulance was coming. Then she went to Mrs Nosey Next-Door and spun her a long story about her mother going into hospital and could she let the ambulancemen in. Mrs Nosey Next-Door couldn't wait to get the key off her and get ready for a poke about. She told her she had to go and get a prescription for her mother.

Then Spuggie packed a little bag for herself, took the ten-pound notes she'd been saving and set off to find Beckett, clutching tight and warm in her hand the chess piece, the hopskip knight itself, wrapped in the plain brown paper it had come in; the plain brown paper which read on the outside HM PRISON LANCASTER. She knew where Lancaster was. She knew how to get there. She'd seen it on the map and the road led straight like an arrow to Carlisle and on to the motorway and then straight down. When she got there, she'd work out how to make them let her see him. She could spin them a story, she was good at that. They could hardly push her away if she told them how far she'd come. She could even say she was his daughter, they'd have to let daughters in and how would they know she wasn't? She caught the bus and watched the countryside go past with a far-away look in her eye. Nothing had anything to do with Spuggie now, not Fraser, not her mam (who was getting looked after at last), not the Grove, not anything except the big adventure she had started, a big adventure that would take her to where Beckett was, where she felt she had a right to be.

Fraser came home at lunchtime and watched, biting his lip, as they put his mother in the ambulance. He couldn't see Spuggie anywhere and he began to worry. He worried even more when he saw the social worker, Mrs Meade, arrive and go in. He didn't know what he expected to happen after that. He didn't think Spuggie would have hung round but he half thought she might have and he wasn't sure what he would do if he saw his sister being dragged off, screaming, into care. As it happens, all he did see was a worried-looking Mrs Meade come out after a bit and drive away. Which made him glad and fearful at the same time. Because if Spuggie wasn't in the house, where was she? School, he hoped. Maybe the Grove; and then another thought came to him. Maybe she'd just stayed in the house and kept quiet. In which case, they had a fighting chance of staying out of care until their mother came home, cured.

He crept into the house and up the back stairs. He was on the landing, fitting his key gingerly into the lock and wincing at the racket, when the door behind him swung open and there was the next-door neighbour, smiling at him.

'Your mam's had to go in hospital, pet,' she said. 'I let the ambulance in.' For all her nosiness, she was a kind soul and she looked at Fraser with real sympathy. 'Kirstie's had to go down the chemist's and get a prescription. Why don't you come and have a cup of tea with us till she gets back?' Fraser thought about this. 'I can make you a corn beef sandwich, as well,' added Mrs Higgins enticingly but Fraser thrust the idea aside.

He not only had to find his sister, he had to find out how his mother was and he had to work out where he was going to hide in case the social came looking again. And then he heard the sound he dreaded. Mr Nosey Next-Door was on the telephone in the hall and from the muffled bits that Fraser could hear, he knew who was on the other end of the line. He shot into his own flat and packed a bag quickly, just enough to see him through a couple of nights. He peeped out, then had another thought. Opening his door wide, he banged it shut loudly, then opened it just a crack and watched while the next-door neighbours came out and wittered. They nearly knocked each other over, going back in to telephone the latest news to Mrs Meade — that he was away. Which he wasn't, of course, but at least he had a bit more time to think about it.

Mrs Meade got the second telephone call and sat down heavily. She knew she had been late getting to the house. In an ideal world, she would have been there, either with the doctor or at least with the ambulance. But, in an ideal world, there would have been more time and fewer cases on her case list. She didn't think Spuggie would be at school. She remembered her determined pugnacious face. Whatever Spuggie had in mind, it wouldn't be going into care. It would have helped a lot if there had been any close relations but she knew there weren't. She rang the school and got the secretary, who sounded as harassed as she was herself but promised to help. Then she rang Geoff at the Grove, who sounded, if anything, more concerned than she was. He promised to help too.

And on the outskirts of town, Spuggie got off the bus and got on another one. She looked back, for an instant, at the town laid out behind her under the warmth of the early afternoon sun and she said goodbye to it under her breath. She wasn't coming back, no matter what.

Fraser did the rounds cautiously. He spoke to Bridie, the closest thing Spuggie had to a mate. She hadn't seen anything. He hung around the Grove, watching the cellar especially closely, but saw nothing. Then he took what little money he had and bought some food to put in his little bag. He knew where he was going to hide.

At the hospital, Robert was beginning to show signs of recovery. His foster mother, Lou, spent as much time as she could with him. Speedy was there all the time, refusing to go to school. Speedy, the usually harum scarum Speedy, was in deep shock over what had happened to Robert and Lou could see how much he was blaming himself and Radio Rocket for it. Wisely she didn't let him off the hook but just listened to what he had to say and let him talk it out, both with her and with Robert.

Charlie had a different problem. She wanted more than anything to be with Robert. The big difficulty was that Steve Rettega had signed her up. She was going to sing on his record, it was going to be released and the only way he was going to get airtime, he said, was if they did it there and then. She didn't know the way Steve's mind worked. Steve had reasoned to himself that it was a real shame that Robert had hurt himself waiting in a wheelchair but it would be a much bigger shame if no good came of it. And so he wanted to make the record and he wanted to have it released and he had a tame journalist and a news photographer and a spot on local TV. But first he had to make sure the record was up to scratch and, he could see for himself, it's hard for a kid to sing with tears running down her cheeks.

So, he went to see Robert in hospital. Lou looked at the medallion, hiding discreetly in the hairs at the top of his open-necked shirt. He saw where she was looking, gave her his best self-mocking grin and shone his big blue eyes at her.

'Listen,' said Steve Rettega to Aunt Lou. 'Do you think I don't know what I look like? This is part of the image, isn't it? If I was a priest, you'd expect a dog collar and a rosary and a holy expression, right? I'm a record producer, this is the way I make a living. I've got to wear chains and look flash or I don't get anyone to take me seriously.'

She looked deep into the blue eyes and she was lost. 'So?' she said. 'What?' she said and Steve told her how he needed Charlie to make a record. She felt her mind closing but he opened it again by pointing out that what was good for Charlie was also good for Robert. The better Charlie felt, the better Robert would feel because she would be coming in here with eyes like stars and a voice like melted honey and if that wasn't an incentive to get off your back, he, Steve Rettega, didn't know what was. Aunt Lou didn't entirely fall for the patter but enough of it got through for her to see that what Steve was saying wasn't all toffee and so she agreed it might be a good idea if Steve had a word with Robert.

Then he went away and picked Charlie up in the flash motor with the mobile telephone and he told her that before she sang another note in a recording studio maybe she ought to go and have a word with her boyfriend, to see what he thought about the whole affair. He dropped her off at the hospital and she went into the little room where Robert was lying as stiff as something nailed to a board and she sat and chatted to him.

'Mr Rettega brought me down,' she said and she smoothed his forehead. He nodded and there was a little bit of flirting and to-ing and fro-ing and they looked into each other's eyes quite a lot which made Speedy want to vomit, peering in through the little window in the door until Lou caught him at it.

'What does she want, coming down here all the time bothering him,' he grumbled. 'It's not as if he wants her here.' But Lou just nodded and smiled wisely. Wait till you catch it, she thought to herself. Just you wait. And Speedy played his own funny brand of hopscotch down the corridor and wished that Charlie would go away and he could talk to his mate again.

Inside the room, things were growing very quiet between the two lovebirds. Charlie had told him that there was going to be a record and he had just nodded and looked away. 'You're not helping much,' she said after a bit and he said he was sorry. Then he explained how low he was feeling and how the record would take her away from him and how he'd heard the specialist tell the sister in charge that they thought he'd have to go away for special treatment. And, to his absolute horror, he felt a tear run down his cheek. But Charlie just bent down and kissed it away. He struggled to smile.

'I knew it'd be like this,' he said. 'When you got me at your mercy.' She grinned and whispered in his ear. What she said has got nothing to do with us but it made him tingle in places he didn't think he'd ever tingled before and it also made him go quite red. She stood back and raised her eyebrows.

'Is that enough incentive to get better?' she said and he nodded, breathing a little harder. Then she had to go because Rettega was waiting downstairs. But Robert wasn't worried about her going. Not now. As she reached the door, he called her name softly.

'Charlie!' he said as she turned, 'I want you to be a *super*star!' She blew him a kiss and went. And the good feeling stayed with him for ages even when Speedy beat him at Scrabble.

And all that afternoon and all the long evening, Charlie

and the technicians and Steve Rettega worked at the song and as the work went on, the faces grew more and more excited and Steve kept exchanging knowing looks with the sound man. They were getting good stuff and Charlie sparkled and bounced and opened her throat again like a blackbird and sang her heart out, putting all the things she felt and couldn't say into the song she was singing. And the ordinary pop song became something else. Something special.

Earlier that day, Hayley had done something stupid. In fact, anyone who knew Hayley would have sworn that she had done it on purpose. Nobody will ever really know, but what she did earlier that day had Michael Warner, Julie's dad, waiting in his car outside Gill's squat, trying, in his own ineffectual way, to find the courage to go inside and see if what Hayley had told him was true.

Hayley was besotted with Vas Takedeli and, far from being the cool dude he normally was, Vas was getting hung up on Hayley. Most of the time, he just did what Steve told him and being told to attract Hayley's attention was a giggle. At first. But Hayley and her big smile and her attitude to life made Vas look once and then twice. In fact he was proud to have her on his arm. Not only on his arm, but in the BMW, the black man's wagon, named after the immortal Bob Marley and the Wailers. That's one of the reasons a BMW doesn't get trashed like other cars. That's what Vas told Hayley, anyway. They were driving along, school having become irrelevant to Hayley, when who should she see but Julie's dad. More than anything, she wanted to be seen by someone who knew her. That's what she told Julie a long time after when everything had changed and they were older and wiser. But on this day, on this fateful day, Vas stopped the car at the lights and Michael Warner looked across and Hayley shouted across and asked him how Julie was. Which was stupid because Julie was supposed to be staying at Hayley's house. And if she wasn't, Michael Warner had a very good idea where she *was* staying.

Now, he sat outside the dismal house with the wrecked car in the yard. He'd been there once before. It seemed like a hundred years ago when Julie had first taken up with the North-Eastern lout he now suspected she was living with. He groaned with indecision and again, for the hundredth time, reflected on the rotten job his wife had made of bringing up his daughter. He was the kind of man who saw things that way. Eventually, he managed to make himself get out of the car and go into the house and up the dirty stairs. He stood, looking at the door, where Carl found him and immediately stood in front of him. Michael looked at him with distaste.

'You're one of Gillespie's friends, aren't you?' he said. Carl grinned at him.

'I might be,' he said. 'And whose little friend are you?' Carl knew very well who Mr Warner was, of course, but that didn't stop him being difficult and objectionable. Mr Warner pushed him to one side, surprised at once by the weight of muscle in Carl's body. Carl gave way, only to see what happened next, and Michael Warner knocked at the door. Julie's voice from inside asked who it was and Michael groaned silently to himself. He raised his voice.

'Open the door, Julie!' he said and there was a silence, Carl coming up close behind him. He turned and pushed at him but this time Carl didn't give way. He pushed back and while they were engaged in a silent pushing match, Julie opened the door. 'Go away, Dad,' she said. 'I'm not coming home.'

Michael Warner reached towards her but she stepped back out of range. Carl caught him round the neck and wrestled him to the top of the stairs, and they rolled down, pushing and wrenching, rather than doing each other any harm. Carl got the older man's neck in a stranglehold and forced him through the door and out into the yard. Julie came halfway down the stairs, her hand to her mouth.

'Stop it!' she shouted. 'Stop it!' But the grim, quiet trial of strength went on. Warner freed his arm and hit out, catching Carl round the ear. Then Carl went berserk, kicking and punching. But before he could do any serious damage, Gill came rushing into the back yard. He saw what was happening and felt sick with rage. This was the last thing he wanted. He dragged Carl away and put all his anger into one stiff, sharp, straight jab right between the eyes. It jolted Gill's arm all the way back to the shoulder and sat Carl down suddenly on the base of his spine, knocking the breath out of him. Julie rushed out and Warner looked at Gill, still trying to catch his breath.

'You can't go on staying with him,' he said to Julie, without taking his eyes off Gill. 'I want you to come with me. Now. And we'll say no more about it. Otherwise,' and he jabbed his finger at Gill, 'Otherwise, he goes to jail. I mean this, Julie. I mean this.' And he sagged against the fence, a middle-aged man feeling every year of his age.

Julie looked at him straight in the eye and told him calmly and coldly that if he ever spoke to the police, he would never see her again. She would just go away. He looked at her implacable face and knew she was telling the truth. He could see all the stubborn determination of her mother – all the things he loved, admired and hated all at the same time – all the things he couldn't cope with. His shoulders drooped and he walked away. Gill put his arm round Julie's shoulders and they watched him go. They both felt sad for him but couldn't raise a finger to call him back.

They had pain enough of their own and it kept them awake half the night, holding each other tight, trying to talk about it, all the time knowing there was no easy way out, knowing that life was catching up with them, that the short happy time was over and not wanting it to be.

Gill worried at work all the next day.

Julie stayed at home and worried, moping round the house and looking out through the windows as the rain

130

speckled down. When Gill came home, they neither of them had much to say. Gill went out for fish and chips and Julie listlessly warmed a couple of plates with hot water from the kettle. When the knock came at the door, she was startled but decided to try and raise the general mood. She arranged a smile on her face and opened the door, crying merrily, 'You're getting very polite all of a sudden.' Then she stopped and stared at her mother who gave her a small smile.

'Hello, Julie,' said Clare Warner. 'I think we've got some things to talk about. Can I come in?' And Julie stepped aside numbly.

About fifty miles away, stepping it out after a long hard day, Spuggie was getting very weary. She had a blister and the last bus she'd caught had dropped her by a little shop where she'd bought some crisps and a fizzy drink and a cake. She hoped it wasn't much further to go. A big black car went past and then stopped and backed up to her. A man leaned out and looked at her.

'Hello, little lady,' he said. 'Hello, nipper. Would you like a lift?' And she looked into the back of the car. Then she got inside and sat back. For the first time, her feet had stopped aching.

CHAPTER EIGHT

Julie sat and looked at her mother in disbelief. Clare smiled back at her a little sadly. There were shadows under Julie's eyes and Clare thought, with sudden pain, that her daughter was too young to have worry shadows under her eyes. And she thought again, a little wryly, that there were probably shadows under her own eyes after the telephone call from her husband and the sleepless night and the long train ride north. She looked around the room.

'Is this what you want out of life?' she said. 'That's not a criticism. I really would like to know.' Julie looked her straight in the eye.

'This is what I've ended up with, Mum,' she said and her mother nodded. She knew that Julie would blame her for leaving Michael and the natural consequence of that was that Julie would see this room as her mother's fault too. She went back on the attack.

'You're not even sixteen yet. And living with a boy who has no prospects. I suppose you're sharing a bed too?' Julie flushed and couldn't meet her mother's eyes. She fingered the plaited wristband and her mother nodded. 'I hope you are taking precautions, then? Because a baby at your age would really be the icing on the cake, wouldn't it?'

This was enough for Julie and she snapped back. 'Is that what I was?' she said. 'The icing on the cake?'

There was a brief pause as Clare Warner felt that shot hit home. She didn't have to reply, as Gill came in just then with his fish and chips, right into the middle of it. His jaw dropped. Clare smiled, taking control again.

'Hello, Gill,' she said. 'Come on in. We were just talking about you.' And she sat them both down on the bed. She knew she had to be very careful. She couldn't impose any decisions on them. They or rather her daughter had to make up her own mind and Clare Warner had to make it

132

look as if it was Julie's own doing. Any other course of action, she knew, would be disastrous. She loved Julie. She wanted her to have a good start in life. But she was going to make sure that Julie chose. She was also going to make sure that Julie chose right. She spoke carefully.

'I want you both to take time to think and I want to take Julie away for a little while,' she said. Julie's reaction was immediate and emotional. She linked her arm through Gill's and hugged him close. Clare looked at Gill and was pleased to see the uncertainty in his face.

He ducked his head slightly, accepting what she said. Julie was cross. 'Can't you see what she's doing?' she cried. 'She's trying to split us up.' And indeed, that was what Clare was trying to do. Separate them and work on Julie and show her a little bit of luxury at the same time. Which, judging from the state of the room they were in, should come as a welcome change. Julie eventually agreed to go back to the hotel with her mother and Gill would join them later for a final decision.

Mrs Meade, the social worker, still cross with herself for having missed the children at the flat and still worried because Spuggie had been missing all day and the previous night, went to the hospital but couldn't get any sense out of Betty Campbell. She was too weak to talk and too confused, anyway. Then Mrs Meade drove to the Grove to talk to Geoff and Mary O'Malley, who probably knew the family best.

'I'm not blaming you,' said Geoff but the social worker shook her head.

'You should be,' she replied. 'I should have been there and I wasn't. Luckily this was the only place where things went pear-shaped.' She packed all her files away as she talked. Then she breathed deeply. 'When she turns up,' she said to Geoff, 'keep hold of her, I don't care how you do it, and give me a ring, OK?' Geoff nodded gloomily.

'Don't you mean *if* she turns up?' he said and she looked at him, shaking her head. 'If I meant "if",' she said gently, 'I wouldn't get much sleep tonight.' He grimaced in apology and she left.

Mary tapped Geoff on the arm. He turned in surprise and she held a finger to her lips as she closed the door and made sure Mrs Meade had gone.

'What?' said Geoff.

'She'll have gone looking for that feller,' said Mary. 'Him that was hid in the cellar.'

Geoff thought about this and then picked up the telephone to ring Grant and find out where Beckett had been sent. He put the question, listened, nodded and put the telephone down. Beckett had been remanded to Lancaster. Mary's face grew longer and more doom-laden. Spuggie would have to go out across the moors to get to Lancaster. They looked at each other and the same thought struck them both. The moors were no place for a little girl on her own. Geoff got up with a new sense of purpose. 'Right,' he said. 'I need Fraser. And I think I know where he'll be.'

He was right. Fraser was in the radio room with all his kit and a sleeping bag. He was talking to Speedy about going into care. Speedy had had the brightest idea he'd had in months. Fraser was worried about being separated from Spuggie.

'D'you want me to ask Auntie Lou if you can come and live at ours?' he said. Fraser looked at him, puzzled. As far as he knew, you couldn't pick and choose where you went if you went into care but, as Speedy went on to say, there was no harm in asking. Robert would be in hospital and there was a spare bed in Joanne's room. Fraser's spirits lifted a little. He knew Auntie Lou. His mum wouldn't be in hospital forever. It might be a real good way out. And then he remembered about Spuggie. He knew exactly where she'd gone. He knew his sister too well and he remembered the look on her face when she was talking about the man in the cellar. The door opened and there stood Geoff. Fraser thought for a moment about making a run for it but Geoff shook his head.

'I've not come to turn you in, son,' he said, and Fraser was ashamed for even thinking it of him. 'Come on,' said Geoff. 'Let's take a belt out the Hexham road and look for this little ginger sister of yours.'

Speedy followed them out, one-track mind burning away. 'Shall I ask Auntie Lou?' he said. And Fraser turned and gave him a big grin. Maybe things would turn out all right after all.

Gill was beginning to think things would never turn out all right for him. He walked the damp streets, head down, as the crowds of early evening teenagers made their way on another Newcastle night out. The skimpy skirts and tight shirts and fancy hairdo's and bright eyes mocked him all the way to the hotel where Julie and her mum were waiting to tell him his fortune.

Julie had just come out of a hot bath and was wrapping herself round a plate of sandwiches. She looked at her mother knowingly. 'Are you trying to soften me up?' she said but Clare shook her head. Julie was too like her to fall for that one and she said so. They sat and munched the food together.

'Nice,' said Julie, peeling up a corner of the sandwich. 'What is it?'

Her mother pulled a face. 'I don't know,' she said. 'But at two pound eighty a go it ought to be very nice!'

And they both laughed until Julie remembered why she was there and thought of Gill and grew solemn. But Clare watched her face and nodded quietly to herself. She could see what was happening.

Downstairs, Gill walked into the lobby and, as soon as he saw the plush surroundings, he knew what was happening too. He was rude to the commissionaire and even ruder to the reception clerk and went into the lift with a chip on his shoulder a mile wide. He knew how to work a lift – he'd got GCSEs. He went into the room expecting the worst. But he got the shock of his life. And he got a sandwich and a cup of coffee. And they all talked long and hard and sensibly about the options for a young couple with no money and no resources. They talked about squats and council flats and housing associations and Gill fought as hard as he'd ever fought for anything to keep Julie with him.

Clare Warner knew what he was trying to do and her heart bled for him. It wasn't that long since she'd been young herself and she could still remember the heartache and the hopelessness that went with puppy love. However, she wasn't young now and she also knew the potential for pain in committing yourself too young to one person. At twenty, you were vastly a different person from your sixteen-year-old self, and at twenty-five just as different again. She let them talk and she listened and talked herself. She didn't offer advice. She didn't offer solutions. She didn't do any of the things you might have expected a mother to do. But, in her own way, she was fighting as hard for her daughter's future as Gill was for her love.

And then came the shock. She stood up. 'All right!' she said. They looked at her uncertainly.

'What d'you mean?' said Julie, looking at Gill.

And Clare spelled it out for them. She was leaving on the eleven o'clock train the following morning. Julie had till then to make up her mind. And she let them both go and when the room door was shut, she sat on the bed and burst into tears. She hoped she'd done the right thing, gambling. But she might never know.

And, as Gill and Julie walked home through the night streets, her mother's last words rang in her ears.

'You made a decision last year,' Clare had said, 'over your father. Now you can make a decision over your boyfriend. *Your* decision. I don't want you blaming me. This is where the growing up really starts.'

136

And, as they walked, each buried in their own thoughts, not daring to say anything to each other, Julie felt terrified and excited all at the same time, sensing the tremendous pull of her own decision-making power, the chance to state her own needs and become her own person.

But all Gill could think of was how much he loved her. And that was always going to be the difference between them.

Geoff and Fraser ploughed up and down all the likely roads in the van until it was too dark to see. There was one point when Fraser was sure he had seen Spuggie down a little lane. He was certain he had seen the lights flash on her red hair and they had driven round and round a housing estate until Geoff had stopped and turned to him.

'I know!' said Fraser. 'I know. We're never going to find her. She could be anywhere. I'll kill her!' And his voice cracked at the thought of his lonely little sister out there on her own somewhere. Geoff patted his shoulder. There were no words he could think of to make the lad feel better.

So, they drove back to the Grove where there was a big strange black car standing in the driveway. Geoff looked at it curiously. It was nobody's he knew and Fraser didn't recognise it either. Geoff had a sudden chilling thought that it might be an unmarked police car and that they might be bringing news of Spuggie. One look at Fraser told him that he'd had the same thought. They got out of the car without saying anything and went into the Grove.

Spuggie was sitting there, surrounded by Mary O'Malley, Alison, cups of tea and biscuits! Fraser could have killed her on the spot.

'We've been looking everywhere for you,' he said. 'I've never been so frightened in my life. I'll kill you!' and Spuggie put her head down and wept. She knew she'd done wrong.

Geoff turned to the man sitting nearby, with kind blue

eyes and an accent with a country burr. He introduced himself as Will Caws from the Isle of Wight. His wife was with him and their two daughters, Sophie and Lucy, big-eyed at the fuss.

'Couldn't let this little nipper walk those moors on her own,' said Mr Caws. 'Mary tried to get her to tell us where she lived but all the address she'd give us was this here.' His wife nodded and, after thanks all round, they made their way off.

Spuggie looked shamefaced and said she was sorry.

I expect you are,' said Geoff 'but we'll deal with that tomorrow. What are we going to do with you two till then?' Fraser said that they could stay at the Grove but Geoff said over his dead body and they agreed that Fraser could go home with Geoff and Spuggie could go with Alison. And Alison could give her a little talk about getting in cars with strangers. Spuggie pulled a face but it made no difference. She got the talking to. She had never seen Alison in such a forbidding mood and it was a very sad and thoughtful little girl who went to bed that night, reflecting on Alison's words.

It's hard to say who had the worst night, Clare Warner in her overheated hotel room, thinking of the darkness under her daughter's eyes, or Julie Warner, lying next to Gill, knowing he was awake and not having any comfort to give him, or Spuggie, in a cold sweat, knowing what might have happened if she hadn't been picked up by such nice people.

The next morning, Clare got up at first light, ate her breakfast and did all she could not to call a taxi and go and get Julie. She read every newspaper the reception desk sold and tried not to look at her watch. But the time passed too quickly and eleven o'clock came with no sign of Julie. She paid her bill, her lips clenched tight, and walked quickly over the road to the railway station. She bought two tickets, one for Julie, hoping against hope. The clock ticked round to departure time and she found her seat. She had to stick to her word or Julie would never trust her again. But as the train wheezed and the whistle blew, she leaped up and started to run to the door, only to come face to face with Julie, the shadows under her eyes deeper than ever. Mother and daughter clung to each other, all the reserve and lies gone from between them. They both cried and didn't need to hide the tears.

'I'm coming with you,' Julie said. 'I can't think with Gill there. Just for a couple of days. All right?' And Clare nodded. And they sat and watched Newcastle upon Tyne and the river and the bridges pass beneath and behind them and away out of sight. And Clare Warner knew that she had won the first skirmish in the battle for her daughter's future. And Julie knew that she was leaving a piece of herself behind in the North-East.

And, later that day, Gill trudged up the alley behind the house where he'd been so happy and so sad, almost all at the same time, past Carl and his sneer and into his lonely squat to find Julie's note, telling him goodbye for just then, telling him that whatever she did decide, she would come back and tell him. He crumpled the note up and threw it away while his emotions fought a war inside him — relief at not having to fight for Julie, desperate sadness that she had gone, tugged him this way and that.

In the hospital, Lou sat by Robert. He was building himself up for his own goodbye to Charlie. Lou looked at him tenderly. With every day that went past, more of the man in Robert came to the surface. So young, she thought, and with such a big weight to carry. He watched her face and smiled to himself.

'I've got to go to the Rehab Unit,' he said.

'It'll not be so bad,' she replied but she knew how far away it was. He nodded and grinned again, trying to keep a stiff upper lip. 'Apart from the fact that it's a hundred and fifty miles off, you mean?' he said.

Her tone became mock cross. 'You want to walk again? Don't you?' And Robert pretended to think about it until Lou tweaked his ear. Speedy came in with a contraband copy of *Viz*. Lou saw it and was outraged, trying to take it off him. They struggled till she got it and squinted at it.

'It's a comic,' said Speedy defensively. She peered at it and decided not to get her reading glasses out for a better look. Buster Gonad, she could make out. The rest she would rather not know about. And then, to Speedy's utter disgust, in came Charlie with a bunch of flowers.

'What have you brought flowers for?' said Speedy. 'He's not dying, you know!' But Charlie was by now much more than a match for Speedy and secure in her feelings for Robert. She just retorted that the flowers weren't for Robert's grave, they were for Speedy's and, while he was still spluttering and looking for a snappy answer, Lou tugged him out by the ear. He protested for a bit until he thought that Lou was feeling sorry for him and then he asked her if Fraser and Spuggie could come and live with them. He didn't know that Mrs Meade had already sounded Lou out and she didn't tell him, letting him think that it was all his idea and a good one at that. One of the things that made Lou a very good foster mother was that she knew how important it was to make people feel good about themselves. Another thing was the way she thought of children as people and not possessions. And so it was settled that the Campbell kids could be part of Lou Gallagher's family until their mother was well enough to look after them herself.

In the hospital room, Charlie bent over Robert and kissed him and whispered, 'Will you miss me? He kissed her back and thought about it and then shook his head.

'No!' he said and she punched him gently. 'Hey!' he said, 'Mind me rivets!' And they held hands until it was time for Charlie to go.

Then Lou said goodbye to Robert and hurried home to make things all ready for Spuggie and Fraser, juice on the table and sandwiches in the kitchen. She knew how important it was to let them come in and settle, like cats in a strange house, sniffing and finding things for themselves. Fraser came in and her heart went out to him, his face small and suspicious, his eyes worried. She wanted to give him a hug but she knew better than that. She told him about the juice and the food and where his room was and let him do it himself.

Spuggie was still in the car, talking to Alison. Mrs Meade had wanted the lesson rammed home about strangers and cars but it had to come from someone Spuggie knew and trusted or else she would just shut it out. In the car, Spuggie looked away till Alison forced her to turn round.

'You were stupid,' said Alison. 'But by the grace of God you were lucky too.' Spuggie nodded. 'You cannot look at someone's face and know what that person is like. There is no way to tell. Do you know how I know?' Spuggie shook her head. 'Because once, when I was a little bit younger than you, I made the same mistake that you did but I wasn't as lucky as you and I have spent the rest of my life trying to forget what happened. Promise me, Spuggie, promise me you will never, ever, find yourself in a position where your choices are taken away from you.'

Alison's words were so strong and so forceful and so full of meaning that Spuggie realised for the first time how stupid and how lucky she had been both with Beckett and the allotment and with the Caws' and the car. She breathed and nodded yes. Then Alison gave her a big radiant smile.

'Right! Sermon over. Let's see if we can screw a couple of cups of cocoa out of this new foster mother of yours.'

And Spuggie looked at her carefully. 'She's not my foster mother. I'm just staying here for a bit till my mother gets better. Then I'm going home.'

Alison bit her lip and nodded and they both went inside. Spuggie had made her point.

*

For a while, life at Byker Grove grew calmer and Geoff, for once, felt better about it. He'd had enough crises to last him forever and all his time and energy were now taken up with the arrangements for that great celebration of North-Eastern youth and high spirits, The Great North Run, which deserves every one of its capital letters and is a chance to show how fit you are if you're young and also raise a few bob for your favourite charity. All the kids from the Grove dressed up as Teenage Mutant Hero Turtles. Geoff was a St Trinian's schoolgirl, Alan Dobson took a day off from worrying about the fast-splitting leeks and tried to break the long-distance drum roll record. And, on the day of the Run, with a heavy heart, Geoff sprinkled purple powder in the cash box to catch whoever it was that was stealing his money.

Alison, despite some misgivings, was sharing a pantomime horse costume with Brad. Against her better judgement, she was in the front and she reckoned she'd be lucky if she finished the race with her shorts still on.

Before they all assembled to get on the lorry to go to the race, Charlie had something important to do. She went to the hospital and watched them load Robert on to the ambulance and just before they drove him away, she gave him her present. It was a walkman and it had a tape in it and he travelled a hundred and fifty miles to the Rehab Unit with a silly grin all over his face and Charlie's voice ringing in his ears.

The rest of the day went well, with a few exceptions. Alan Dobson broke the drumming record, the Grove kids made a large amount of money for charity and Alison changed places with Brad and pulled *his* shorts down, which made him say they'd better get engaged. And Geoff, to his eternal dismay, found Duncan desperately trying to scrub purple powder off his hands in the boys' loos. But, Geoff being Geoff, was able to solve that one too.

So there's only one end to tie up, really. The days passed slowly and bitterly for Gill. Pay nights, he drank as much as he could afford. Other nights, he looked at Julie's photograph till his eyes grew red. Several times he rang her father but always put the telephone down without saying anything.

And then one day, he went to answer a knock at the door and there stood Julie. It was a new Julie, who'd grown up more than he could ever have imagined in the time she'd been away. He tried to put his arms round her but she gently eased them apart.

'I thought you'd gone for good,' he said but she just shook her head. And he knew what she was going to say.

'I've only come back to say goodbye,' she said. 'I didn't want to do it in a letter. I came back to see you. And to say goodbye to Newcastle.'

They went and sat by the lake they had always loved and looked at the water and Julie tried to explain to Gill what she needed.

'I'll never forget you,' she said. 'But I've grown up. I want to do things. Go to university. If I stay here with you, I'll never do any of it.'

He looked at her sadly, knowing what she was saying was true, angry but understanding at the same time.

'I'm not good enough for you,' he said. 'That's what you're saying.' But that wasn't what she was saying at all.

'I'm not good enough for *you*,' she cried, desperately wanting him to understand. 'I'm too selfish. I want more than you can give me.' She paused and a wave of tenderness and regret swept over her. 'Kiss me goodbye, Gill!' she said. And if he had, maybe the ending of the story would have been different but all Gill could do was shake his head and hide his tears and stumble blindly away. And Julie watched him go and she would remember that moment all her life.

And the remembering began as she sat in the train and watched the lights of the city disappear. And she remembered all the good things, all the warmth, all the friends,

143

everything that Newcastle upon Tyne had given the spoiled little schoolgirl from Wimbledon.

And she remembered that very special place.

She remembered Byker Grove.